TREASURE
IN THE
SAND

TREASURE IN THE SAND

ANDRÉE T. PARENT

ARPress
45 Dan Road Suite 5
Canton MA 02021

Hotline: 1(888) 821-0229
Fax: 1(508) 545-7580

Ordering Information:
Quantity sales. Special discounts are available on quantity purchases by corporations, associations, and others. For details, contact the publisher at the address above.

Printed in the United States of America.

ISBN-13:   Paperback   979-8-89389-556-8
              eBook   979-8-89389-557-5

Library of Congress Control Number: 2024920613

Table of Contents

To my children

Sophie, Manon, and Philip,
and my grandchildren
Jacob and Emmanuelle
I am grateful for all the encouragement
you have given me.
Your MOM

Picture by Andrée T. Parent
Tortola, B.V.I. Taken 2007.

Chapter One

Andrea Karr was sitting in her favorite chair hanging from a high beam on the veranda of her cottage home in the Virgin Islands. The veranda was facing the clear blue water of the North Atlantic Sea. It was a beautiful twilight night for a mid December evening; the reflection of the full moon surrounded by stars was dancing on the water. A soft gentle breeze caressed her bare shoulders as she lifted her head towards the dark sky and saw a bright shooting star.

> *"Star Light Star bright,*
> *The first star I see tonight,*
> *I wish I may, I wish I might,*
> *Have the wish I wish tonight."*

She closed her eyes and uttered her wish out load. "I wish the last two weeks of my life never happen."

She opened her eyes and watched the shooting star fade far away behind the mountains, tears came rolling down her face realizing even if she could wish on all the stars in the universe nothing would erase the last two miserable weeks she just experienced. Her darling James was gone forever. Every night since that day, she sat on the veranda for hours powerless and unable to move, crying herself to a point of being inconsolable and sick to her stomach.

Every night since, when Andrea finishes with her crying, she would go over the events of that horrible day. She would start from the moment they woke up that morning to the exact minute of when it happened: his death.

"Why would someone deliberately run him over? It does not make any sense!" Every night she would arrive to the same conclusion.

Not one person on that street corner who was present that day can give her a definite answer of what they saw or what they heard that happen to James.

She would call the police department several times a week and their reply was always the same:

"Please let us do our work Ms. Karr, we will get in touch with you if any new details or information is brought forward to our attention, we promise you will be the first to know." The Detective Pondas add replied.

She also interrogated all the merchants around her store, and they said the same thing to her.

"We do not know more than what we have told you and Ms. Karr you were also present that day." They all informed her.

That day, they were referring to the 3rd day of December 2008, in the middle of a normal workweek when the life of Andrea Karr changed forever. Andrea and her husband James Woods were a very loving, happy young successful couple. They lived together ever since they married in June 2006 at Long Bay Beach, Beef Island, Tortola.

Their home is situated forty minutes from Charlotte Amalie, the capital and largest city in St Thomas, of the U.S. Virgin Islands.

With the ferry, which operates a state-of-the-art high-speed catamaran, sails service located at the other end of the deep-water harbor it makes it a nice peaceful ride home morning and night. The harbor is also renowned for its international port of call. At one time, it was a legendary sanctuary for pirates of high seas. An estimation of 1.5 million passengers from cruise ships, pleasure boats and seaplanes moor every year and a third of those visitors are during the Christmas season, which it makes it the busiest season of the year.

On that morning, the town was buzzing with activities more than usual and all the merchants had open there shops earlier to accommodate the hundreds of tourists just arriving for the day.

Andrea herself being the owner of a well-established Arts and Antique boutique situated in the Market Square was very successful. It had made her the most thriving businessperson of the year for two years consecutive.

Some nights she would arrive at home well past midnight and some other nights she would sleep on a small cot in the back room of her store, too tired to drive home. The local artists support all the stores in the small town.

One time she had told her sister "The people of the island work hard to make a decent living with little of what they have. I try to buy everything locally to support them and during the slow season, I employ one or two citizens to help me clean the store from top to bottom. I love this place and the people; I am very grateful to have a small business and be accepted by these wonderful people."

Nevertheless, her sister did not agree with her, she begged Andrea to move back home to Canada with her and her husband

This year everything was different, she did not look forward to Christmas season or the festivities. Saying her goodbyes to her sister Kelly, and her brother-in-law, Jonathan, yesterday morning at the airport was too much for her. They were the last to go after the funeral. Her sister had insisted on staying behind for a couple of weeks, but Andrea had refused, she knew when the time came for Kelly to leave her it would be that much harder to find herself alone again. Her sister begged her to come for a visit in the New Year, but Andrea was determined to find out what had happened to her husband and why. She promised herself she would not stop until all of her questions had received an answer and then she would start thinking of moving back home but not before.

Now at the end of this day and every following day after for the rest of her life she would need to face them alone without him. Sitting there admiring the night sky she drifted into a shallow sleep. She woke up several times during the night has Charlotte, her cat, would jump on her knees at the sound of dogs barking in the distance. She narrowed her eyes to see better her watch only to realize that just a few hours had passed. She would close them again and slowly falling back to sleep. She slept the entire night on the veranda, once again. As she opened her eyes slowly, she felt the humidity on her face and bare arms. She tried to uncurl her legs slowly, but they were too numb from being tucked underneath her all night. She remains in her chair a few minutes longer, admiring the fog lifting over the water, the waves crashing against the shore, the cry of the seagulls for the dead fish floating in the water and in the distance the sound of music coming from the morning jogger's iPod. This was her favorite time of the day when the beach came alive. Slowly rubbing her legs, she eventually managed to get up and walked back in the house.

In a few hours, she will be re-opening her antique shop on Sunny Street. The store had remained closed for two weeks and now she had to face everyone especially the ones who came to the funeral to pay their last respect to James. The cemetery was full of friends and customers; people they had met during their few years together and people whom she had never met before, mostly clients of James from other islands.

Now she was a widow, people would look at her differently; they would ask her questions about; have they found the man who ran James over? Will she be selling? Will she return to Canada now that James is dead?

How can she face her friends with no answers? How can she accuse one of the islanders of murder? Yes, murder, Andrea been informed with certainty that James Woods, her husband, was murdered.

She found herself with no answers to give them. She shook her head as if to clear her mind. She needed to concentrate on things like, taking a shower or getting dress for the first time since her return from the airport.

It was now eight o'clock on a Monday morning and entering the city, already crawling with tourists. The store situated on the corner of the first street coming from the peer; it was the perfect location; her colorful store was what attracted the tourist in. The building painted in pink with beautiful hand painted flowers of the Island and a sea blue trim was shaping the form of different windows. Some people like her sister and brother-in-law would say it looked awful, others would say it brings joy to the corner street and stands out as a landmark.

"Look at all the other buildings around here, they are painted in similar pastel colors, and this makes people curious to come in and see what we have to offer inside. It's good business to be flashy on these beautiful sunny islands." She had happily replied to her sister on her first visit to the islands.

Her shop was furnished with trinkets, clothing all made by hand with also antic pieces of furniture, precious stones, art, and hand weaved rugs. Some of these pieces were brought by James from other islands during his business deals. Millions of travelers each year would venture from the security of their ship to go on outings, such as, the beaches, boutiques, restaurants to take pictures and buy souvenirs for their loved ones. The small statuettes or art print, sun hats were small enough to carry back to the ship, rugs, and furniture she would offer to ship them back for a small fee. Others would only have their photos taken in front or inside the store, but they always remembered the small pink corner shop with blue trim windows and return on their next cruise.

She was now turning onto her street when she saw remnant of the yellow tape left behind with the white chalk on the pavement from the accident scene of two weeks ago. She could see the store from where she had stop, at the corner streetlight, and could not bring herself to go forward. People behind her were sounding their horns, still she could not move. Two lights later, she decided to go forward by the back way reaching the side street and stopping at the coffee shop to get her morning Java and toasted egg sandwich. Locals were sitting on the sidewalk patio drinking their morning brew when she walked past them without making eye contact, she didn't feel like greeting anyone, reaching the front door, she directly went to the ordering counter.

"Will this be all Andrea or will you be ordering your lunch at the same time as usual." The young clerk replied with a big smile.

"No thank you Gina, just the breakfast sandwich and coffee today."

Instead of ordering her lunch, she had brought her own sandwiches, two-day-old leftovers from the funeral meal.

A few minutes later, she had finished her breakfast, cleaned, and put away all the dishes in the back room, fixed her hair and makeup and was ready for her first customer.

The week before Christmas, ships and planes where never in port before mid mornings. Waiting behind the store counter, she stared at the window seeing James waving at her from the other side of the street. She closed her eyes, trying to get the image out of her mind but looking out again she knew the corner would always remind her of James waving back.

No matter where she is in the store, there was a moment where James had stood talking to her or holding her in his arms making plans for the future or waiting for her after work to go to their favorite restaurant. All of these moments were coming back to her and she realized now they where only memories and she started crying.

"It was a stupid accident, a hit and run accident, the police officials insist on calling it a murder, a well executed hit on James."

The investigation revealed a diversion was created at the other end of the street by a driver running the red light, screeching his tires to attract attention during that time on the opposite side of the street a white car came barreling down striking James who was standing on the corner waiting for the crossing light to change.

He had called her an hour before from his office at the other end of the city, to invite her for lunch. He mentioned he had a big surprise for her. He always gave her a gift when he successfully landed a big commission from the sale of a house. He was finally making a good living with the selling of properties and this year was the biggest year since he had joined Santomas Real Estate co.

James had worked his but for a couple of years now for Nick Santos a native of St Thomas and the owner of a well renowned Real Estate firm. This year he had been promised a full partnership with his own branch in the city close to Andrea's store, they were both every excited about it.

At the time of the accident, James was the only person standing close to the curb with one foot of the street ready to cross. She watched him from where she was standing in the window of her store ready to go to him. He saw her looking at him and gave her a big smile as she waved back at him. In that split second, from the corner of her eye she saw a white car; she turned her head to see better and saw it accelerating towards James. She looked back at James to worn him and he was already looking at it. He steps backward and bumped into a tourist stepping on his foot, which in return the man push him forward, he steadied his footing but it was too late, he was on the pavement in front of the incoming car. He looked at her with a scared expression, lifted his hand and waved her goodbye: she always wondered did he know his killer.

The driver accelerated and hit him head on. James flew in the air, the driver kept on driving without slowing down. She could not believe her eyes when the car hit James, instantly he flew several feet in the air then dropped on the pavement like a discarded rag doll no longer wanted by a spoiled child. Everyone started screaming at the driver but he did not even look back, he just continued and escaped into one of the side streets of the Market Square. She quickly ran outside across the traffic, pushing everyone aside. When she reached him, she kneeled beside him, carefully picked up his head in her hands and gently placed it on her lap.

She immediately started talking to him to let him know she was by his side, and everything was going to be all right. She remembered her voice was shaking and high pitch and in slow motion. She could not stop saying his name.

"James, James, wake up, James please, please darling don't leave me. James it's me Andrea."

She could not even see his face it was so bloody, his feet and legs all mangled underneath him, and his hands and arms were all scraped and bloody. One bone was protruding from his left arm. She turned towards the tourists and pleaded with them to call for an ambulance, but they just stood there, everyone just stood there looking at him, and at each other not knowing what to do or who to call, then, a voice came from out of nowhere and said.

"Ms. Karr the ambulance is on its way" replied the person.

"Thank you, thank you" she manages to say without even looking up to see where the voice came from.

"Did you hear that darling, the ambulance is on its way, please James answer me." He looked at her with emptiness in his eyes.

She tried to reassure him, but his eyes and mouth were bleeding so much, she could not keep up wiping it off from his face. There was blood coming out from under his body she could feel it soaking her dress. She tried to comfort him by saying everything was going to be all right. "Hang on dear, they're coming, please James hang on, please stay with me, don't… James… do not leave me.

Slowly she could feel him slipping away; she closed her eyes and kissed him on the forehead, tears were rolling down her face as she said her final goodbyes as she forced herself to reminisce with him as when they had first met.

"James don't leave, please don't leave, we just started our lives together, remember all our plans we talk about." She reminded him about those beautiful moments they shared together; she could hear the ambulance siren in the background she looked up at the people around them. He squeezed her hand and slowly he let her go, it was too late, he was already gone.

The next day in the local newspapers a short story was printed.

It red like this:

A hit and run in the streets of Charlotte Amalie.
A local business
Man, resident and husband, James Woods, was hit by a car yesterday on the
corner of Sunny Street and Main, at twelve fifteen p.m. Mr. Woods died
at the scene a few minutes later. If anyone has seen the accident and can
supply information about the identification of the driver or the car, causing
the accident, please get in contact with the local policia at 313-626-9999.

Beside in another column of the same paper from a different writer, he wrote. {*A hit and run on a local businessperson caused doubts into the minds of the policia and the residents. Who and why would someone do such a thing to a citizen of the island? Could this be another mystery of Charlotte Amalie?*}

She had phone the police department regarding the news clip. She wanted an explanation of what did they mean by another mystery of Charlotte Amalie.

"We will send someone over to see you shortly."

Before long, a detective came to see her.

"How can that be, it's an island, a car just doesn't disappear in thin air? Why can you find this specific car or the driver?"

"Hola Sonora their is nothing we can do" said the Detective;

"It was done so fast, and the car disappeared quickly. Many citizens came forward with information, but they were incapable of giving a decent description of the car or the driver. Now all the visitors from the Cruise ships are gone, and locals, well if they saw who it was, they are not talking, Ms. Karr. We will keep you in touch if we have new information regarding this investigation."

Soon after their talk, he left her all alone in the middle of her store: It was the day after the accident when she returned to the store to post a sign in the door.

CLOSED FOR TWO WEEKS FOR PERSONAL REASON

Ever since that day, she has been calling every day for information and in return, they requested her to stop calling.

She keeps replaying over and over the events of the accident in her mind ever since. As she forgotten any important details? Remembering James flying in the air makes her cry and loose control every time so she decided one night to write everything down on paper this way, she would not need to go over every night to keep it fresh in her mind for the next time she has a meeting with the officer and wants information.

Andrea had met James a week after she had moved from Quebec Canada in January 2005. James Wood was also a Canadian from Vancouver and had been a resident of the Island since year 2000. When James first arrived on the Islands, he was hired as a bilingual tourist guide for the City of Charlotte Amalie and a promoter for the yearly carnival. It was at one of those many events they had met. She had just arrived from a long stay abroad with her girlfriend when they decided to pass a year on the island and work their way back on Cruise ships. One day while apartment hunting, they stopped at a local bar, The Paradise Point, where he was organizing a scavenger hunt. Their eyes met and they immediately started talking. He had told her; the guide position was a temporary job until he receives his real estate agent license that he was studying for and pass later that year.

They had dated for a while, later that year when her best friend returned to Canada, Andrea stayed behind, had moved in with James, and later they married in June 2006. This year was going to be their third Christmas together

When people would see them together on the Island, they would refer them as the inseparable snowbirds from Canada. The only time they were apart, would have been when James went on trips promoting tourism for the city or showing houses on other islands for the agency, and never more than a fourth night. Everything was going well for them.

Today, she was alone, no husband, no friends close by no sister and now the Holiday season just a few days away, how she will survive the end of the year.

The last two weeks she has passed it with her sister and brother-in-law sitting on the veranda reminiscing about their last visit, James was so happy. They talked for hours lounging outside looking at the stars, eating and drinking wine planning their next visit. On the visit she kept asking her sister why someone would want to kill him and what was so important he wanted to tell her that day. What was the big surprise he had for her?

She was daydreaming when startled by the phone ringing and she let out a scream. Charlotte the cat who was lying across her desk fell on the floor and ran to the back of the store.

"Sorry Charlotte" replied Andrea. She always brought her cat with her at the store. The cat came into their lives on their second date. They were walking on the peer and saw this poor scruffy baby cat curled up in a ball and shaking at the sound of people footsteps. When Andrea saw the poor animal tried to pick it up and the cat scratch the top of her hand. She manages to appease the cat and decided to keep it and decided to name it Charlotte after Charlotte Amalie, Queen consort to King Christian V of Denmark. People just loves Charlotte; she brings a live-in ambiance in store.

Has she picked up the phone, the voice at the other end greeted her in Spanish.

"Hola! Senora Karr?"

"Hola! Si. This is she.

"Cómo está usted?" He continued in Spanish.

"Muy bien" she replied. "Tū hablas inglés?"

That was the extent of her vocabulary in Spanish language without humiliating herself. After almost two years, she never took the time to learn Spanish mostly because the people on the island spoke English or English Creole, Spanish was the third language and rarely people would talk it.

"Si, I speak English.

"Oh! Hello Detective Pondas. I am sorry I did not recognize your voice. What can I do for you?"

Detective Pondas was one of the first officers on the scene of the accident with the ambulance when James was killed.

She was attentively listening to what the man had to say to her with an expression of wonder on her face.

"Why?" She asked. "Why? Is something wrong?" She asked with concern. She repeated and he kept evading her question by asking her more questions.

"No, I don't know why he went to Great Camanoe Island on that day, maybe he was there to sell some property, did you ask his partner Nick Santos, at the Santomas agency, where James worked?"

"What?" She could not understand all these questions and why on the phone.

However, the man kept insisting on asking her questions that she had no idea of what he was talking about, and he kept saying Spanish words that irritated her. She was constantly asking him to repeat himself in English and he was getting frustrated with her.

"Meet with you? Why, where, when… today! Yes, all right I will meet with you…at the station at what time! Not at the police station? Where then? Yes, I know the place, yes, at one thirty I will be there, Long Bay Beach, Beef Island, at the West end. Ok I will be there. Goodbye Detective Pondas."

The man hung up and she felt confused and worried about what he wanted to talk to her so urgently.

She looked at the clock and started to get ready for her meeting, place the close sign in the door and left. Long Bay Beach was about forty minutes from the store by the Queen Elizabeth Bridge. During this time of the day, the ferry is at it busiest with tourist going to the beaches on other islands meanwhile the roads are mostly clear, so, she decided to go by that avenue.

"Why would he want to meet with her at Long Bay Beach, it's so secluded and the beach is two miles long, why? Is it because I live their?" She wondered.

Forty minutes later, Andrea decided not to go home but to drive directly at the Bay Beach parking lot. She parked her vehicle at the far end and looked for a police cruiser, a man in a uniform or a man dressed in a suit, but all she saw was two cars parked at the other end, a navy-blue car and a black van. She looked up and down the road, waiting. She decided to go on the beach to wait for the officer. She walked over the space between the trees over the sand dune that separated the parking lot from the beach. She came out on the other side and placed her hand over her eyes to search better the beach. From left to right see looked and saw no officers or Detective Pondas. She noticed a couple sunbathing and about a few feet from them a mother with her baby playing in the water and a man standing half waist in the water fishing, otherwise the rest of the beach was deserted. It is always quiet and peaceful in the middle of the day, especially a few days before Christmas.

This was James favorite beach. As soon as they moved here, every other weekend they would spend hours on the beach playing ball and swimming.

They had plans to own a bigger lot at this end of the beach where it is more private, and the flowered trees are bigger and more beautiful.

She had started to walk towards the west end of the beach towards the mountain when she noticed someone lying in the sand all dressed. She walked slowly always looking at the person expecting him to get up at the sound of her voice calling him, but the man stayed undisturbed, she approached carefully. Has she got closer and closer to the person, she noticed he was more rigid than a normal sunbather would be, and his clothes were wrinkled, and his skin was more bluish than tan. The minute she reached him, she noticed he had papers stained with blood on his chest.

She started screaming uncontrollably as she approached him and saw the man was dead. He had his eyes opened; blood was coming out of his mouth and ears. The couple near by started to run toward her when they heard her screaming like a crazy woman. Has they approach and saw the blood on the man's face; they stopped and looked at her and try to calm her down.

Then the man and the women with her baby also started running towards them, the woman beside Andrea waved to them not to come forward. After she had calm down, she reached for her mobile phone in her purse and the Detective Pondas card he had left her on the day of the accident and immediately called his office.

"Hi, may I speak with Detective Pondas, please." This is Andrea Karr." She announced.

As she was surveying the beach and looking towards her house for anyone who would look like an officer, she was surprised to hear his voice when he answered.

"Yes, Detective Pondas here".

"Detective Pondas, this is Andrea Karr, why are you still at your office."

"Hola! Senora Karr, what can I do for you" replied the Detective.

"What can you do for me? I am at the beach waiting for you! There is a man here lying dead on the beach where you told me to meet you!"

"What? I do not understand, what do you mean; you are waiting for me on the beach? I never called to arrange a meeting with you, Ms. Karr, what are you talking about?" he replied confused.

"Did you or did you not call me this morning to ask me to meet with you here at Long Bay Beach for one thirty?" She sounded furious with him and now her voice was trembling. "No, sorry I was here all morning giving introduction courses to our new recruits. What is wrong Ms. Karr, what is this you are saying; there is a dead man on the beach." He sounded impatient with her.

"Yes, a dead man, please come quickly" I will explain to you more clearly when you get here."

"Where is here?"

"You know, where I live, Long Bay Beach, at the other end of the beach!" She pointed without realizing he could not see her gesture.

She hung up the phone and started talking with the couple close by. After everyone had finally calm down, she managed to get information from them; they mentioned seeing the man when they arrived and did not wanted to disturb him so they decided to go at the opposite end of the beach with their young child.

"He looked as if he had slept their all night, we didn't pay any attention because we figured he was a local who had too many drinks last night and was sleeping it off on the beach." Replied the fisherman.

It was more than half hour before they could hear the sirens of police cars approaching. The first one to arrive on the beach was Detective Pondas. She started walking towards him when he lifted is hand and motioned her to stop where she was and signal to the officer that accompanied him to follow him.

He passed by her without greeting her.

He approached the body alone and examined it carefully without touching it, while the other officer gathered pieces of what may be evidence in the sand. He slipped on a pair of rubbed gloves that he retrieved from his jacket with several small plastic bags and started to go through the man's pockets. He found a wallet, keys, and several book matches. He looked inside the man's wallet to find information regarding who he might be, he found the man driver's license, red the name, studied the man face to verify his identity and placed it neatly back in one of the plastic bags and handed over to the young officer. He picked up the papers that had now slid of the body resting in the sand.

He turned towards Andrea and motioned her to come forward.

"Ms. Karr, now tell me who called you?" He continued is questioning by a series of other personal questions… If she new this man …if she had touched anything and why did she leave these papers on his body. He repeated. "Are you sure, you didn't touch anything and these papers." He was waving them at her. "They are not yours." He kept on insisting.

"First, don't you ever say Hi? Or Hello! To people. Second, no, I do not know this man and I did not leave any papers on his body. They were already on his chest when I arrived, and I did not touch anything. Yes, I am sure and again…I never saw this man before. How many times should I repeat myself? You can ask these people, they were here before me and has seen me arrived, the man was already lying on the beach."

"Ms Karr just because you say it, that you do not know this man it doesn't mean I believe you." Again, please look at the man face."

She was now mad at the Detective for doubting her and making her look at the man again.

"See I am looking at him and no I don't know him." She looked at him very fast and returned her gaze to the detective. "Why should I know him?"

"You do not recognize this man?"

"No, who is he?"

"This man is Nick Santos, the part owner of Santomas Realty with your late husband"

"No, what are you talking about? That is not Nick Santos, because I know Nick and his wife, and this is definitely not Nick. It does not look like Nick at all."

"Ms Karr, please look carefully at this man and honestly tell me that you do not believe this is Nick Santos!"

She slowly stepped forward, closer and closer to the body and carefully examining the man face, as she remembers exactly what Santos features and his eyes deep brown eyes look like, he was a beautiful man, this person had similar features but the expression of fear in his eyes were more like James eyes the second before he was killed.

She looked carefully at his nose, his mouth, afterward his chin and soon realized this man could be Nick Santos.

"But he is dressed as a bum and has a deep tan, almost burnt face and heavier more like bloated." She remarked.

"Yes, he is burnt by the sun and bloated by the time he spent in the water, which is normal."

"Oh! No." She started to cry. She kept stepping backward and shielding her eyes with her hands and repeatedly, "No, not him…no please, not Nick also, why is this happening?"

She then turns towards the Detective and pointed to the body.

"Yes, this… that." She pointed to the lifeless body. "I believe it is Nick Santos. But why would someone call me and pretends to be you and asked me to meet him here?"

The man, who called you, has you known was not Nick Santos but maybe the man responsible for his death. Did he introduced himself as me; did he say this is Detective Pondas? Try to remember Ms. Karr."

'The only thing I remember is he kept talking to me in Spanish and I told him I didn't know Spanish that well and he got annoyed with me. Why would he killed Nick Santos and then call me to meet him here where he discarded the body?"

"You tell me Ms. Karr" the Detective replied with a sarcastic voice.

She looked at him with a puzzled expression. "What are you trying to imply? That I know who killed this man, Nick Santos?"

"Maybe!"

"Well, I do not and you can go to hell if you think I am capable of murdering someone, I swear, you do not know your business, he was already dead when I arrived, asked them." She pointed to the young couple talking to the other police officer close by.

He looked at her for a long time, studied her body language, and then replied.

"No, I don't think you killed him, but I would not be surprised if you knew who did! This man, Mr. Santos, was killed a few days ago, dump in the water and washed ashore maybe late last night or early this morning.

"You mean I may be involved with the person who did this to him? You are kidding me, yes. Why would I be involved with murderers?"

"I don't know yet, but I will find out. I am sure your husband played a part in this man's misfortune, and without you knowing or having anything to do with it, you may know who did it."

He paused studied her behavior for a few seconds and returned to look for more clues, footprints, cigarette buts or burnt matches. Anything that he saw he took a picture and then picked up and through it in a plastic bag with the other articles that the young officer had found.

"Mrs. Karr! Are you sure the man said my name, Thomas Pondas when he called you this morning when he fixes a rendezvous here on the beach!"

"I don't know, like I said, I assume it was you once he started talking in English."

"No Mrs. Karr you said the man introduced himself as me, Detective Pondas or did he say Detective Thomas Pondas.

"Well, I am not sure if I remember him saying your name, or I assumed it was you."

"Or maybe it was the killer, or maybe wanted to tell you who killed your husband or maybe he wanted to kill you also, and, when he saw Santos body he got scared." He mocked.

She looked at him and screamed. "You still have nothing on my husband murder and on top of that you are assuming that I am involved with all of this, what kind of detective are you?" She looked at him angrily and began to cry. She could not believe after three solid weeks of crying; her eyes could still produce tears.

The Detective gave her a handkerchief and resumed his questioning.

"But really how much do you know about this man? Can you tell me when you and your husband saw Nick Santos last, Ms. Karr?"

She wiped her eyes and then blew her nose in his handkerchief and handed it over back to him.

He looked at it and replied. "That is ok, you can keep it, and you may need it again."

"Thank you". Without realizing what she had done, continues.

"James, last month, told me Mr. Santos was bringing is wife to Europe for the Christmas season and they would not return until the end of January. He had planned a Paris New Year for their fifth anniversary and then, continue to a Villa in the French Riviera." Still emotional she added. "He left James in charge of the offices."

"Yes, but, when did you see him last." The Detective insisted.

"I!" She took a deep breath and before she could answer.

"Yes you Ms. Karr, when is the last time you saw him." He cut her off. She looked at him with disbelieving eyes.

"I saw Nick and his wife…last June at my birthday party. James gave me a party at the Blue Moon Café in Charlotte Amalie. We were four couples. You can verify it if you want" She suggested.

"Oh! I will." He replied with a mocking tone in his voice.

The Detective just realized he was still holding the papers he had found on the body. He quickly gave a second glance through them, turned towards Andrea, and shoved them in her hands.

"I believe these belong to you, your name his written on them."

She looked at the papers without touching them and replied.

"No, I don't think so…the papers where on top of him when I arrived. As I said, I did not place them on his body. What are they?"

"It looks like a deed to a lot on this beach" I will need them back to check if they are legal and for evidence."

"Why did you say they belong to me then?"

"Andrea T. Karr is your name!" He looked at her and she nodded yes.

"Well Andrea T. Karr is the name written on top of the first page of this contract has, owner of lot 56 on Long Bay Beach located at the west side of Beef Island. Blah, Blah, Blah," he continued.

"What does that mean?" she questioned him.

"The only lot I, we, purchased on this island is at the other end where we lived for the past three years. Maybe my husband bought the lot for me just recently? He told me the day he died he had a surprise for me, maybe he wanted to give me this property."

"Maybe or maybe not" I will get in touch with you Senora, you may go now."

"Where is lot 56?" she inquired looking around the beach.

He pointed toward the sunset at the end of the beach.

She looked where he was pointing and there was nothing but trees and a small mount of sand.

As she turned to walk away, he added in a loader voice.

"Ms. Karr, please do not leave the islands, and please provide all the phone numbers where I can reach you." He touched his eyebrow with his hand and dismissed her.

She looked at him tears rolling down her cheeks. Where does he think she would run? As she reached the parking lot, sat in her car for a few minutes wiping her eyes and instead of going home she decided to return to the store and finish her day. As she was, making her way to the waterfront highway she stopped the car on the side of the road, wiping the remaining of her tears, fluffed her hair and took a deep breath to regain the little of composer she had left.

"I can do this." She persuaded herself. She pulled back onto the street and noticed in her rear view mirror a light color car following her in a distance. After a few minutes, Andrea arrived in the parking at her store, looking at her watch she noticed it was close to past four o'clock and she felt her stomach growling and a headache coming on. She decided to walk at the corner deli to pick up a sandwich and a beverage. While waiting to pay for her food she glanced out the window and spotted the same car passing slowly in front of the cafe. It was not odd to see the same cars passing over an over again in these small narrow streets, tourist got lost every day, but this was not a rental car circling around in the city trying to find there way out to the beaches. Returning to the store, she found several people looking through the windows to find out if the store was open and pulling on the doorknob. She noticed she had the wrong sign on the door.

She unlocked the door made her excuses to the tourists and welcomes them in, answering all their questions regarding the city and the story about her own store.

The rest of the day went by fast and uneventful to her surprise.

At seven o'clock, a wave of fatigue came upon and decided to close the store early. Has she been closing shoppers were still coming in to buy souvenirs at the last minute before returning to their ship, by the time the last customer left it was now closer to eight o'clock and police cars were passing more frequently she noticed at least every half hour. She did not know if that made her feel safer or more uneasy. She closed all the lights except for a small lamp on the counter beside the cash register, turned the close sign to face the outside and slipped out by the back door into the parking lot where she descended slowly the stairs and afterwards ran to her car.

Chapter Two

A few days as passed since her encounter with Detective Pondas on the beach. Drinking her morning coffee, she went over every word he had said and promised her: "I will call you back in a few days."

Well, a few days have pass, it is now Christmas Eve, and why was he not calling her with information regarding the progress on the case? Her husband's death still listed as unsolved, if the detective has information about James' case, he should contact her, Christmas Eve or not. Two suspicious deaths related to the Santomas Realty within a month, made everyone uneasy. Could the killer still be on the island like the detective said, or did he dump the car and escape on one of the cruise ship?

Twenty-fifth of December, Christmas day, she received an invitation to join her neighbors for a swim/party on the beach. As an Island tradition, the locals gather every year on the beach for a full day of parting, fun, food, and dancing. She accepted has they would have if James would still be alive. After just few hours, she could not take it any longer and excused herself from the festivities. She returns home, wanted to write what people had told her about James and what they had seen right after her husband accident, also why a stranger has been asking information about James, if he was dead or injured. She wrote everything down and placed it under a refrigerator magnet easy to see and read every time she would open the refrigerator door. She wanted to make sure she did not forget a thing.

All the information she has gathered and other questions about Nick Santos, Mrs. Santos, James, and the agency for the next time they meet.

- First, did Nick fell off his boat and drowned or was he dumped in the water after he was killed? Did the Detective know for sure what happened?

- Second, did Mrs. Santos return from Europe with Nick, if so, does she have any answers about her husband's death?
- Third, should she contact Mrs. Santos regarding what to do with the partnership?
- Fourth, where was she when Nick died?
- Fifth, why are they not looking for her?
- Sixth, did they speak with her?
- Seventh, why people are being killed and for what?
- Last, how is James involved in all of this?

"I have all these questions; someone needs to answer them." She had told her sister on Christmas morning; she would not return home until she was satisfied with answers.

It is Boxing Day now and yet no calls from Detective Pondas. She took the list and placed it on the table, and she decided it was time to call him. She started dialing when she looked up at the wall clock.

"My goodness 7:00 a.m., it is much too early in the morning to call Pondas, he wouldn't be at his desk this early the day after Christmas."

She could call just the same and leave a message, but she refuses to talk to anyone else for having to repeat herself regarding James accident. She picked up the list, placed it in her date book, under the 26 of December, and wrote:

- Call Detective Pondas,
- pick up stamps
- mail thank you cards
- Unpack James boxes- donate or sell content.

In addition, she wrote other important things she had to do during the course of the day.

She decided on leaving early and without breakfast. Unexpectedly for a holiday, the ferry was empty; the commute was rapid. She did her morning ritual at her favorite café, ordered her special day treat, Danish with side order of goat cheese and a café Latte instead of her usual egg sandwich. She was convince that today was going to be a good day until she came out of the coffee shop and noticed a bigger crowd of people than usual gathered around the newsstand beside her store.

Walking slowly, she saw the side of her building covered with red and black paint. As she approached closer, the black paint became more visible to the eye, and she could visualize forms of letters painted in red.

"Good morning, Samuel" she saluted the newspaperman has he extended his hand to give her usual bundle of different newspapers from around the world.

"Morning Ms. Karr".

"What's going on Samuel? Did some kids write graffiti and my wall again? She asked has she turned to face the wall.

She dropped her papers, breakfast, and her coffee on the sidewalk as she came face to face with a blown-up picture of James accident and Nick Santos drowned body from the beach. Beside the pictures, written in big black letters with red contour was.

"SHUT UP OR U NEXT"

"Who did this?" As she turns around to face the small crowd on the sidewalk, she pointed to the wall.

"Did someone call the police regarding this?" She was now looking straight at Samuel.

"No ma'am... can't you read? It says: Shut up or U next".

"No one wants to be next," said another man standing beside her.

"I know what it says." She turned abruptly to face the man beside her. "I can read, and I am sure it's not met for you! Did someone call the police?"

Everyone started shaking their heads and walking away leaving her standing alone facing the pictures on the wall. Tears started running down her face at the site of James blooded face with his eyes opened staring at her. She stretched on the tip of her toes to reach the picture: has she pulled to set it free from the wall, she lost her balance and scrapped her hand and wrist against the brick wall and almost fell backward when someone caught her.

"What are you trying to do? Can't you read, what it says?" said the voice behind her. "And you are destroying evidence, this is a treat or possible of another murder.

She turned to face her savior to find this tall, beautiful person with big dark eye staring at her.

She quickly responded: "Leave me alone, I am not afraid of you"! I am calling the police. Do you understand me, let me go."

He grabbed her by the arm so hard that, she felt the pain and tried to jerk it out of his grip. He forced her close to him. She could feel his breath on her face.

"Ms. Karr stop, stop it."

She flung her other fist directly at his mouth. He grabbed her wrist in mid air; she looked up at him with tears in her eyes, ready to receive her punishment.

"What is the matter with you?" He screamed at her.

"Leave me alone, let me go". She was pushing him to get free of his hold on her wrist.

"I will let you go if you stop acting like a child and listen to what I have to say to you."

Her eyes were wide open and staring at him.

"See that note on the wall!" He pointed to the brick wall behind her.

"Yes" She slowly managed to mutter the word out.

"It's not a joke! People like that do not joke around for the fun of scaring young widows."

She stared at him powerless and unable to talk.

"I am letting you go." Slowly he released his grip on her.

"Do not make a scene. You do not want to attract attention to yourself; you don't know who might be watching!"

He picked up her breakfast bag, coffee and papers, handed them back to her and winked, he turned the corner, and he was gone.

Did he know her well enough to talk to her like that? She could not place him if they had met before. Was he a client of James? He did not look the type of person to scare young women or even killing them. Was he a friend of Nick or Mrs. Santos?

"More questions!" She whispered.

She unlocked the front door, immediately pick up the phone and dialed Detective Pondas number, as she waited to be transferred to his office line someone walked in the store. She looked up and Pondas was standing there in front of her.

"Hi! I was just on the phone with your office." She explained.

"Good morning Ms. Karr."

"We were busy this morning decorating." He replied with a tone of sarcasm referring to the outside wall.

She ignored is comment and replied." What are you planning to do regarding that, and also I received the visit of a man who was harassing me about it."

"You have received the visit of someone regarding the message on the wall."

"That is what I just said. Why would someone try to hurt me, I have not done anything wrong? What do they want with me? The wall is not damage; a good coat of paint will fix that."

"Are you sure you are not withholding information from me Ms. Karr?"

"What information?"

"What was your husband's business?" I mean is job, any past time, or hobbies? Ms. Karr".

"Detective Pondas you very well know what my husband's jobs were!" He worked for the city of Charlotte Amalie as a tourist guide and for Nick Santos as a Real Estate Agent for over two years and recently made partner."

"Yes, but what did he really do in his spare time?"

"What are you implying Detective?" Are you trying to say my husband add a third job that I didn't know about!"

"Ms. Karr a double homicide was made in my city, and I don't like it at all. You come clean and tell me every thing that you know right now. I also want the listing of every house your husband ever sold and where they are located from the day he started with the Agency and a list of all the people you both know."

"I can't do that; I know it is impossible for me to know everyone he knew. Why don't you ask the agency, they would know more than I about the houses he sold in the past two years?"

"Well, you better find out who they were, because the agency is closed and all the furniture is gone, and, we can't find Mr. Santos widow. Would you know anything about that?" He asked her directly.

"No. I don't know her that well except for the few times we saw each other, I did not socialize with them."

He looked around to see if someone was in the store shopping and then said in a very low voice.

"Ms. Karr can you follow me outside, please, I would like to show you something."

"Yes, certainly but first I have a few questions of my own to ask you."

"You have questions? Regarding what may I ask?"

"About James, Nick Santos, Mrs. Santos and the agency for example?"

"Not again. Ms. Karr please."

She ignored his comment and started by:

"I have list right here in my book." She retrieved the list and started.

"First, Nick Santos, did he fell off his boat and drowned or was dumped in water after he was killed."

He listened very patiently, and she continued.

"And the Real Estate agency, who will take car of it, will it be sold?"

"Well, I ..." he tried to answer.

"You said you cannot find Mrs. Santos, does anyone know if she is back from Europe? Did you speak with her maid?" She kept on going without letting him answer a single question.

"She may have answers about my husband's death. Should I contact her regarding the agency?"

"Who, the maid?" He was now getting all confused with all the questions she was throwing at him.

"No not the maid, Mrs. Santos." She looked at him wandering if he was paying any attention to their conversation or was, he preoccupied with something else.

"Stop with all these questions, I will answer them when I have the answers. Please come with me."

He gently pushed her sideways as he passed in front of her to reach for the door; He opened it and she started to walk out when a white car with tinted windows drove by and the person sitting in the passenger seat threw a pop bottle and shouted insanities at her. The bottle hit the side of the door broke into pieces and hit her on the arm and leg; she screamed at the noise it made when it came in contact with the door, the Detective drew is gun thinking someone was shouting at them. She backed up inside and stepped on Pondas foot.

The car drove away and Andrea shaking sat down on the floor crying.

"Are you ok Ms. Karr?" He extended his hand to help her up from the floor.

"Yes, I think so." Lifting her hand towards him, she realized her arm had smeared blood down to her wrist. She immediately examined herself and saw blood on one arm. She swiped the blood with the other hand and instantly screamed with pain and more blood came rushing down faster.

"Wow that hurt, no I guess I am not ok, I'm bleeding, and I believe I have glass inside my arm; I will need your help to remove it, please hurry it hurts"

The Detective reached for his handkerchief wrapped her arm and grabbed her by the hand and lifted her up from the floor onto her feet.

"Come, I will bring you to the hospital."

"No, no." She replied. "I am ok; I will go by myself later just remove the glass inside and I will bandage it."

"I insist, you could have more than a piece of glass in that wound. And you will need your two hands to maneuver your car later; you would not want to hit a tourist."

She looked at him with hanger in her eyes for having said that, but she knew he was right.

"Yes, you have a point; I think I will need some stitches."

She picked up her purse, placed the card in the window and locked the door.

The card red: [Back in 15 minutes]

He looked at her and then the card again. "15 minutes don't count on it; it takes longer than 15 minutes just to navigate through the traffic today. Several Cruise Ships have arrived early this morning."

"Oh no, I will lose a lot of business if I go to the hospital now, I really need the business with James being gone."

He looked at her, shrugs his shoulders, and opened the door, this time he walked out first in front of her and then extended his hand for her to come out. She accepted his hand and they walked to his car parked on the side of the building.

Andrea and the Detective did not exchange words during the long drive to the hospital, on the arrival at the emergency he started questioning her about what she saw.

"Well, I saw exactly what you did Detective. A white car with two people at least driving slowly in front of my store, screeching the tires, throwing an empty bottle at my door and screaming words at me." She looked at him funny.

"What about you, what did you see?"

"I am the Detective of this case Ms, I do not answer questions.

"Well, you know what I saw, and no, if you're going to ask, I do not know them!"

"Thank you, I will fill out a report, the doctor will stitch your arm now I will come back for your later, to drive you back to your store."

An hour later, Thomas entered the examining room and found Andrea ready and waiting.

"The cut was not too serious I trust; did you need sutures?"

"Yes, I got three sutures and a tetanus shot just in case. Thank you for asking."

As they walk back to the parking lot. "Ms. Karr!" the Detective started by saying and then pauses to choose his words carefully.

She turned to face him and saw real concern in his eyes.

"Ms. Karr, this time you were lucky. They might not miss the next time"

"What does that mean, you are the second man today to worn me about THEY and what do you mean the next time? I haven't said or done anything to people, and I do not know what happened to Mr. or Mrs. Santos." She picked up the pace, reached his car, and waited for him to unlock it.

He went beside her gently took her arm in his hand. She pulled away. "What do you mean the second man today?"

"Yes, a man came up to me when I was trying to remove the photos on the wall and carefully warn me. "People like that do not joke around for the fun of scaring young widow and left.""

"Look Ms Karr, you better listen to what he said, that people who write treats on walls usually they mean it. Just be careful and do not venture too far from home or your store alone, that's all I have to say." He started to walk away. "Ms. Karr the man of this morning did you ever saw him around the city before."

"Well, I am not certain." Why should I have?"

"Remember what I said. Ms. Karr."

When they arrived back at her store, she was mad and slammed the door. " Detective, before this happen today, you wanted to show me something outside, what was it?"

"It's not important now." He replied.

"It is to me, it almost got me killed." And she slammed the car door.

Back at the store, she cleaned the glass on the sidewalk and the mess on the wall. She looked up the number of a painter in the local phone book dial the number immediately. Was he able to come today, she needed the exterior west wall of her building painted? He replied he had a free hour after 5 o'clock and he would come by to look at it. What color would she prefer for her wall?

"Well, it's a brick wall and the front is painted pink so maybe a color that would look good with pink." She had informed him.

While waiting for the painter, Andrea started remembering what she had said to James about how they had met and how much happier she was since he walked in her life, well it was not the case now, she was living hell on earth now. She had traveled all over the world, lived in Europe and finally one day stopped here and stayed. The quality of life and security she experienced with her husband was Paradise on earth. Her success she owed it all to him... He had found little shop several months before they met, he had talked to the owner, an older woman who was ready to retire, into selling it to him. When Andrea saw it, she wanted to buy it from James a few months later after they were dating. He decided to rent it to her with option of buying it at a later date. She insisted on paying him every month towards the price of the sell. In order to create a profitable deal, they both agree to conclude the deal before the end of 2007.

At the end of November 2006, James told Andrea, she didn't need to pay him back the balance she owed on the store because he was doing very well with the real estate agency, and he was making enough money to support them both now that they were married. She accepted it, only if it was as a Christmas gift and not charity. She explained to him by doing so, she felt more in control of her life. Now looking around her store admiring what she had accomplished since made her happy. When the doorbell chimed, she looked up and saw the painter.

"Hi! I made an estimate for the wall outside" he commented. "It will need two coats of paint and the pictures what should I do with them?"

"Please just bring them with you and burn them."

It was past seven o'clock when the painter came back in the store.

"I am finished, it's late and I will come back tomorrow to verify my work and for the money."

"Ok, see you tomorrow, thank you."

When he left, she locked the door behind him, gathered all her papers, pick up her purse and left by the back door to the parking lot.

It has been almost two months now since the accident. She woke up to a sunny morning and for the first time she felt happy. Her day started with a small breakfast on her veranda facing the ocean, the sun was warm, and people were already swimming. Last week still, she had been looking for reasons to stay in bed and pull her covers over her head, but now, she finally realized living alone was not has bad and found security again in her daily routine and her work.

She decided to place an ad in the local paper for a part time person to replace her during lunch hours and weekends. Every thing was going fine she could afford some time off from the shop, put her life back in order, and concentrate on finding her husband's killer by herself.

On the Thursday, a local student came in for interview regarding the position of assistant. It was a young girl of eighteen willing to work weekends and odd shifts during the week. Andrea explained what to expect as salary and the hours with her duties, what she expected of her regarding politeness and honesty towards the customers. Andrea informed the young girl; the job was hers if she wanted it since she was the only person that applied. The young girl was excited and ready to start that same weekend.

Andrea was looking forward to having a few hours of her own to be able to sit quietly her desk and pay her bills without constant interruption by customers. She was very pleased with the young girl she hired.

Saturday morning Lana, her assistant, arrived on time as promised, Andrea was able to start working at her desk at eight thirty sharp. It was now ten thirty and she was tackling the last envelope, has she pick it up she recognized the return address; it was a street close of her store and she remembered James had said the owner was living on that street. She quickly opened the envelop wondering what the woman wanted. Inside she found an invoice for two hundred dollars with an explanation:

From December 1ˢᵗ, 2008, to
February 28ᵗʰ, 2009.
Rent for 10123 Bolder Street Apt. G. Charlotte Amalie.
Payable on the 1ˢᵗ of each month. $200.00 cash.
Balance owing $600.00. Payable immediately.
Mr. Woods please advise me if you steel need the loft
over the garage for the month of March 2009.
Thank you, Mrs. Medina.
309-567-4132.

"What is this, James was renting a small apartment on Bolder Street, and paying her in cash on the first of every month." Andrea was shocked and could not believe what she was reading. The woman also inquired if James was still interested in renting the apartment for March and if so, he was late with the rent payment.

"Why James would keep an apartment in the city without telling me." Her curiosity took over her and she picked up the phone, dialed the number from the bottom of the invoice and waited for someone to answer.

"Mrs. Medina, this is Andrea Karr calling, the wife of James Woods".

"Yes dear, I know James, I wrote him a note, and will he still need the apartment, if not I have someone else who would like to rent it."

"Mrs. Medina can you tell me why James was renting the apartment? Was it to store supplies for the store or the agency?"

"I do not know dear, why you don't ask your husband."

"Mrs. Medina, James was killed a few months ago, that is why you did not see him or received payment from him."

The old woman was quiet for a second and then replied. "I am so sorry I did not know about your husband, my deepest condolences. If you come by, you can decide if you want to keep it, and send me the rent money before the end of the month." She informed Andrea with no further explanation.

"Mrs. Medina, I don't have a key for the place, would you have a spare key to lend me until I decide what to do with the apartment?"

"Yes dear, just come by my place tonight and I will give you a key, I live in front of the apartment."

"Ok, thank you, I will be there after six o'clock."

Andrea replaced the phone receiver on its cradle and gave her undivided attention to the rest of the papers on her desk. She did not want to speculate why James was keeping an apartment from her. She let Lana leave early for her first day at work and continued her paperwork until it was time to leave.

At six o'clock, she was getting ready to place everything away when she heard the door chime rang again. Usually, she loved the sound of it, but not today, not when she was ready to leave after a long day. The sound came from a big cowbell on a rope hanging from the ceiling just low enough for the door to hit it when it swung open. Andrea looked up to see who it was but could not see anyone. She continued what she was doing and heard footsteps near the front window; she got up and started walking towards the front desk, wandering if a late customer was shopping for something special.

The day before, Andrea had rearranged the store with Lana and had placed a huge dresser sideways facing the door. This would serve has a double purpose: a dresser to store blankets and pillows as well as a small wall between the front part of the store and her desk.

As she turned the corner of the dresser, she came face to face with the man from the sidewalk. She automatically grabbed her arm still sore from his grip the other day on the sidewalk.

"Hi! Andrea? May I call you Andrea?" He extended his hand to her.

"Hi, what can I do for you?" She was now blushing from his closeness and the way he used her name.

"I was wondering if I may ask you a few questions. Did they found the driver of the white car who hit your husband?"

"Excuse me, why would you want to know and who are you?"

As she noticed, his hand was still extended to receive hers. "My name is Joe Puccino."

"Mr. Puccino what can I do for you?" As she in return gave her hand.

"You can answer my question, if you please!"

"And why should I? You can go to the police station, and they will tell you everything about it, if there is something to tell."

"I will start again: my name is Joe Puccino, Private Investigator." He offered his hand to her with his business card.

She looked at it and spoke. "Mr. Puccino, Private Investigator? I have nothing to say to you, and I have no idea for whom you are working for, also you can tell them to leave me alone."

She looked at him remembering how tall he was, with his dark hair and deep brown eyes, almost black, with an expression that made you look away for fear. He was very well dress, she observed for a private investigator. Business must be good she said to herself.

"Well then Ms. Karr should I leave you alone?"

"What?"

"Ms. Karr, Andrea… since your husband is deceased that makes you, my client."

"Why would I be your client? For what purpose would I need a private investigator?" She asked.

"If you have time, I can explain exactly why your husband hired me and tell you why I was coming to meet both of you on the day he was killed. That is why I was on the scene of the accident that day. Don't you remember I am the one who called for the ambulance and told you they were coming?"

"No, I don't remember you personally, but I do remember someone telling me that everything was going to be alright, and the ambulance was on its way. That was you?"

"Yes, it was." He looked at her with a smile.

"Well Mr. Puccino, has you can see everything is not alright, everything couldn't be worst." She shouted back at him.

"I'm deeply sorry about your husband, but I need to talk to you about what I discovered for your husband. He had a specific request."

"Why would my husband…"

"Ms. Karr…Andrea…May I call you Andrea?"

"I guess"

"Andrea, your husband asked me to…"

At that moment, the doorbell rang, and several tourists entered. She rushed to the door to intercept one of the tourists coming in.

"We are closing, sorry."

'Oh! Please, just for a minute we will be very fast, you are the last Boutique opened and we need souvenirs, our ship sails in a few hours."

She looked at Puccino, turned around towards the woman and said:

"Ok, but you have only ten minutes to look around and to buy something. I need to close the store."

The woman was very grateful and motioned the rest of the group to enter.

Puccino was not too happy with her decision. He wanted to clear up that matter of which her husband had hired him as soon as possible and return to the mainland.

"I will return tomorrow, Andrea!" "Same time ok with you?"

She looked at him and nodded yes. She returned her attention to her customers, and he left.

Chapter Three

An hour later, she was finally locking up the store. She decided to exit by the back door where she had parked her car. As she was preparing to engage the car in drive, she remembered her appointment with Mrs. Medina to check out James's apartment. She removes her key from the ignition place her bags on the back seat and locked the car. She noticed a few boards missing at the far end of the parking lot and decided to try to go through it instead of walking around by the sidewalk. This would bring her directly to Bolder Street as directed Mrs. Medina. She came out in the back of a Groceteria. She looked around to see what street number it was. 10100 Bolder was the number on the face of the store. She searched for her bill in her purse.

"10123 Bolder Street should be close by. Now which way, is it left or right."

She took a few steps forward to check on each side of street to situate her position and if she needed to go up or down the street. As she was checking the numbers on the houses, she noticed a parked car at other end of the street, it was a white car, and she froze in her steps. Was she becoming obsessed with all the white cars on the road?

She decided to go the opposite way; she started by walking slowly and then faster, a few minutes later she found the house on her left. She stopped and composed herself before knocking on the front door. She took a deep breath and turn around to see if the white car was still parked at the same place, she looked on both sides, he was no longer their. She knocked again on the door and then several times, waited but no answer. She wondered if she took the information of the address wrong, or maybe Mrs. Medina taught Andrea had forgotten about their appointment. As she was ready to leave, she decided to go by the back and see for herself where he was living and found the back door was open. In the back yard, she found a double car garage and a set of stairs along side going to what looked like a loft. She wondered if that was James apartment.

She went up a few stairs and then decided to turn back and knocked at the back door of the house instead. She saw a small woman sitting at the kitchen table, she looked at Andrea and summoned her to come in.

"Mrs. Medina?" Andrea asked the old woman as she opened the door.

"Yes, come in dear. You must be here for the apartment key, you are late?"

"Yes, my name is Andrea Karr; Woods, James Woods was my husband, I am sorry to be late it could not be avoided."

"I am sorry to hear about the death of your husband." The woman offered Andrea her hand in condolences.

"Thank you."

Will you be keeping it, dear? Your husband has many boxes and furniture in the apartment."

"I am not sure if I am going to keep the apartment, Mrs. Medina. Maybe not! Now that I am alone, I need to be careful with my money, and I have plenty of room at the house to keep everything there."

The women looked at her with a smile and handed her the key. Andrea did not know what to say to the old woman, so, she thanked her for the key and has she proceeded to go out, the old lady explain it was the first door at the top of the stairs over the garage.

She climbed the stairs slowly trying to image what she would find behind the door. Another life, one of James had forgotten to mention, or was it just a few miscellaneous items of his bachelor days that he did not want to get rid of.

Why did he not tell her? What about the agreement they both made on their wedding day, no secrets from the past, present, or future?

She turned the key slowly and pushed the door open. She entered slowly scared to find something unknown to her. She was surprised, the apartment was furnished with quality pieces and very stylish, the place looked very clean. On one side of the room, a stack of boxes piled against the wall. She looked around no bedroom, just one great room with a leather pull out sofa, big comfortable chairs and a small dinette table with four chairs. A refrigerator, stove, dishwasher and microwave arranged at the other end of the apartment next to the bathroom. It was very well-designed suite to accommodate a bachelor.

She opened every cupboard, looked inside the stove, in the refrigerator she found beer, wine, sodas, and in the freezer compartment there was a bottle of expensive vodka, gin, frozen dip, crab legs and lobsters and a few bags of crushed ice?" In the cupboard beside the stove, she noticed snacks, crackers, and wine glasses.

"What was he doing here? Entertaining women?"

Standing in the middle of the place she started crying uncontrollably to the idea of James being unfaithful to her while entertaining lady friends in his private place. For the first time since James's death, she was mad at him: not because she missed him or because she did not know who he really was, but what he was doing behind her back.

She opened a bottle of wine, found a glass, corkscrew and a bag of chips, sat on the plush grey area rug. She chose one of the boxes and started to look inside it. She stayed in the apartment for a long time.

Inside one box, she found knickknacks, the kind that would bring good money at the store.

"Why was he keeping them here, were they of sentimental value to him?" She said with a sniff.

She also found a box of papers, some looked very old and important, and others were maps of various places, and papers from the Real Estate agency.

"These may be helpful for Detective Pondas to continue is investigation?" At last, she taught.

As she was perusing through the stack of papers, she noticed the address on one of the envelopes. James was using this apartment as an office for meeting with real estate clients. She also found tourist booklets, diving for treasures booklets on different Islands, especially booklets on the Anegada shipwrecks and the Island of Great Camanoe.

An hour later, she was down to the last two boxes. She hesitated, mainly because she knew it would contain the same as all the other ones. She looked at the bottle of wine it was almost empty but just enough for another glass. She decided to finish the bottle and attach the last two boxes.

She noticed one of the boxes had more tape than all the other boxes. She decided to look for a knife in the kitchen drawers, in one of the drawers she found a map of the British Island with red circles at different places in the ocean, she placed it on the counter and returned her search for a knife. She finally opened the box and inside was documents, bills, and more maps, going through them she noticed her name was on several documents, some resembled the one left on top of Santos body, and she also found an envelope also address to her with her. She looked inside and found letters, pictures, and a note about a key.

She also found a deed that she owned not one but three lots on the island including were she lived. All of them, ranging from one acre to several acres, and all were facing the ocean, attached with a clause allowing buildings small cottages to large hotels on each lot. While studying the papers she noticed the lots were purchase at the same time he signs the store over for her.

"Why would James buy lots on Beef Island and never tell me about it. Did he win money? Was he planning to surprise me with these papers on our anniversary? Why would he keep this apartment secret from me?"

She realized that she did not really know James Woods, not the James Woods she loved and married three years ago.

She continues to empty the box and found a small rusted metal box with a key inside. The key did not look like a house key or a security key for a locker or bank volt, it looked more like a key for an old wooden chest or maybe another small metal box. She remembered selling a trunk chest to James before they were married. He had come in one day when they were just married and had bought this brown chest decorated with carvings of pine nuts and trees on the lid.

"It's for my mother!" He had said.

"She is a collector of old trunks, suitcases, crates and toy chest."

She looked all around the apartment, and she could not find anything resembling a chest. Probably he shipped the chest to her after he bought it and forgot to give her the key. She looked again in the small metal box and found an old, yellowed paper with numbers on it.

L26.13.56

L34.65.7?

She could barely make out the last number, it was so faded out, but when she squints her eyes and brought it to the light, it definitely looked like the number 8.

She replaced the paper and the key in the small metal box and placed it on the kitchen counter.

It was getting late, and she had to walk back to her car, she gathered every thing that could be sellable in her store and repacked the rest of the papers in the boxes. There was no phone in the apartment to call a mover, therefore, she would have to go back to the store and make a call right away to arrange for everything to be shipped to her house.

She washed and replaced the glass she had taken and put away the chips and disposed of the empty wine bottle, grabbed her purse and the small metal box and she shoved in her pocket.

She would have returned the apartment key to Mrs. Medina, but it was late and she needed to call the movers before nine o'clock. As she started to walk away, she heard a small voice from the back door.

"So have you decided to keep the apartment dear?"

"No, that's right, I do not need it. I will have someone pick up everything tomorrow. Is that ok with you? I don't know why James needed it unless he was entertaining clients?"

"Yes dear, he was, many people came and went on a daily basis to see your husband."

"What do you mean every day?"

"Yes, every day, women, men, lost of people."

"I had to clean every day the place. Mr. James was very nice to me. He gave me a big storage box for my trouble, come in and see it is in my kitchen." The old woman opened the door and Andrea walked in, in one of the corners, she saw a pile of clothes on top of a beautiful wooden chest.

Andrea went closer and lifted the clothing to reveal to her surprise the wooden chest she had sold James that day. He had said he wanted to buy the first big article sold in her store. She recognized the lid with all the beautiful carvings it was the same chest.

"For is mother he told me! The rotten liar."

"What dear? Who is a liar?"

"No one Mrs. Medina, I am just talking to myself."

She bent over to check the latch; she could not remember if she had given James a key that locked the lid. There was no key hold.

"What is this, another mystery? When will it end, and where does this key fit and for what?" She mumbled.

"Mrs. Medina tomorrow men will come and get the boxes from the apartment. Is that ok with you, will you be here to let them in?"

"No problem I am always here but tell them to come to the back door. I cannot walk to the front door fast enough. What about the furniture?"

"The furniture is not yours?" Andrea asked.

"No, it belonged to Mr. James."

"Keep it, it goes well with the apartment, and I am sure James would have said the same thing."

"Thank you, thank you dear." The old woman looked genially pleased with Andrea's decision.

Andrea took six hundred dollars from her purse and handed it to the old woman. "My I have a receipt for the rent paid, please.

"No, keep your money, please, I am sure the furniture is worth much more than the rent money owed to me, and for the month of February I have already someone interested, and, because of the furniture I will be able to ask much more for the rent. Thank you."

"No, thank you." She said and left the old woman place close to nine o'clock; she wanted to rush back to the store before closing time. Daylight was almost gone, and she was not ready to brave the same route in the dark by herself in high heel shoes. She decided to take the long way back to the store.

Ten minutes later, she was unlocking her store and noticed a white car coming towards her. She rushed in and slammed the door behind her. The car drove by slowly and then turned the corner and disappeared.

Her heart was racing so fast she could not stand up: she had to sit on the floor and lean against the door. It took a few minutes before she got her nerves back to stand up and able to reach her desk. Slowly her heartbeat returned to normal and was able to look up the phone number of moving companies in the area.

"Yes sir, for tomorrow, the address is 10123 Bolder Road, and it's in the back on top of the garage. It is a small loft. You will need to ask the key from Mrs. Medina the property owner, you need to go by the back door. The only things moving are the boxes, seven or eight boxes to be delivered at 1563 St. Marteen, at Beef Island, Long Bay Beach. What? You do not deliver on Fridays at Beef Island. But, Sir, it's only 45 minutes from here by ferry?"

The man on the phone was very persistent.

"Ok, just deliver every thing to this address, 3939 Sunny Street corner of Main. You do deliver on Sunny Street?"

They negotiated a time, and she was not happy with it, but she had no other choices if she wanted to be done right away.

"Yes, seven o'clock tomorrow night. I will be here."

It meant she would have to stay at the store an extra hour just to wait for the Movers.

She finished her call, closed everything for the night and decided to return home.

The 40-to-45-minute commute to and from she enjoyed, especially if she took the ferryboat, she found it very relaxing except for today she could not relax, to many things had happen. Turning on her street, she notices car lights behind her, she turned into her driveway, the car following past by slowly and then accelerated. Her heart started racing wondered if the car was coming back.

"Who keeps following me? If it is that Private Detective James hired, I will give him a piece of my mind. Why would someone follow me, I have no information?"

She slowly parked her car inside the overhang beside the house. She turns off the lights and car engine and waited several minutes in the dark.

She opened the car door slowly and with her house keys ready in her hand, she started running for the front door. She quickly opened the door and closed it behind. She double lock and leaned against the door, waited a few minutes if she could hear a car drove by. She felt like a fool to be so scared of people she does not even know. Why would James put her in that position, did not he love her? She was tired of being sick to her stomach about worrying about her safety. What did she do that was so bad to deserve all of this?

That night she could not sleep, every cracking noise was making her jump. Then she heard a dog in the distance barking, she sat in bed and listen until she could not keep her eyes open.

The next morning, she woke up with the sound of her shutters banging against her window. The sun was already shinning in her room, and she realized she overslept. Usually, she is up before daybreak. She looked outside her window and realized there was no wind, so what made the shutters bag against the window, or was she dreaming? She rushed in the shower, minutes later she was in front of her mirror combing her hair and applying lipstick. She reached in her closet for a dress, what she pulled out made her drop it to the floor. The sundress was very beautiful, with lots of colors; the dress was the one she had on the day James died. The cleaning tag still attached to it, she returns it to the closet, and was ready to grab something else, and changed her mind, James was no longer here just part of her past. She slipped the dress on, reached for her favorite heels, her purse and she was out the door in a record time.

Driving along the coast she realized she had forgotten to eat, and her stomach was growling. She stopped abruptly, when a car cut her off and from the corner of her eye, she saw something flew on the floor. At the next corner, a small restaurant called Hibiscus, located on the shoreline just before entering downtown, she decided to stop at that restaurant and treat herself to a good homemade breakfast before rushing to the store. When she parked the car, she looked for what had flied on the floor, found the small metal box she had shoved in her purse the day before. She placed it back in her pursue and forgot about it.

The small diner opens just for breakfast every morning from five am. to one pm. She chose a window seat that overlooked the marina; she enjoys watching rich people parking their big yacht and sometimes wishing she was one of them and leave on the open sea for months. She noticed two men were descending from a beautiful yacht talking and pointing out to the sea. One of the two she recognized, as Detective Pondas talking to a younger male looking familiar to her. She was curious, how a detective could afford such a big yacht, maybe it belongs to the other man. She finished her breakfast and started for the door when the two men entered the diner. Detective Pondas saw her first and saluted her. The second man with a red baseball cap went straight for their table without acknowledging her presence.

"Where did I see that man before?" she murmured to herself.

"Ah! Well," She paid her meal and left the diner.

Once at the store she had a few quiet moments to herself before her young trainee Lana started working. The young girl was very dedicated to learn about customers and client relationship. Andrea had wondered if she had made a mistake hiring a young teenager, but Lana was serious in her work and eager to learn, she had told Andrea that her dream was to own a store just like this, one day.

During the lunch break, Andrea decided to leave the girl alone for a few minutes to order both their lunch.

Half an hour later, when she came back, the young girl was crying and saying that she did not want to work for her anymore and was heading for the door when Andrea stopped her.

"What is it, what is wrong Lana? Why are you crying?"

"A man came in…she started sobbing…and…he told me to watch my back if I decide to continue working for you."

"What? What man?" By then Lana was really crying her eyes out.

"Lana, please stop crying I can't hear what you are saying when you cry."

"A white car stopped in front of the store and a man with a red baseball cap and sunglasses came inside and said: If I wanted to see my next birthday, I should stop working for you and watch my back."

"Ok, this is it!" "I had just about enough of this." Andrea was furious.

"My God Lana, sit down and stop crying, I will fix this stupid nonsense."

She picked up the phone and called Detective Pondas number.

"Detective Pondas, this is Andrea Karr, please call me as soon as possible it is utmost urgent. Thank you."

Andrea tried to console the young girl and convinced her it was just not true, nothing was going to happen to her if she continues working for her. They both finished their lunch and manage to continue working without interruption.

It was not before three o'clock when Detective Pondas returned her call.

"Ms. Karr what is so urgent, may I ask?"

"You ask what is so urgent, I will tell you, what is so urgent, I just hired a young girl to work for me on weekends and she just had her life threaten in my store by a man wearing a red baseball cap and driving a with car."

"When was this?"

"It was a few hours ago, around noon…ish."

"Noon…ish? What time is that, noon…ish? He asked.

"It's around twelve or twelve thirty or so."

"Then why didn't you say that? Canadians! You are always inventing words." Replied Pondas.

"OK, ok, what are you going to do about it?"

"Why is the man still there? If not, there is nothing I can do right now!"

"Detective Pondas, I have a young girl crying her eyes out since this happen and she doesn't want to come back to work for me. I need you to come down here and tell me exactly what your plans are for dealing with this matter. It has been long enough. I need answers and security of mind for my employee and myself. Do you understand me, Detective Pondas?"

After hanging up the phone, she was still mad and the girl in the store looked at her with big eyes and replied.

"You sure know how to talk to Pondas, Ma'am." Smiled the young girl.

Andrea looked at her and smiled back. "Let's get back to work."

Six o'clock came around, she asked Lana to lock up, and she thanked her for staying on a little longer with her.

Seven o'clock came around and no movers, her stomach was growling since the past hour, should she risk going to the café and miss the movers or wait until they leave. The phone rang minutes later; it was the movers informing her they had arrived at the apartment already loading the boxes to be delivered tonight.

"You have the address where to deliver the boxes?" She repeated the address, "3939 Sunny Street, corner of Main, one street over from where you are."

It was just before eight o'clock when a knock on the door made her jump. She looked through the window and saw a big truck in front her door. She opened the door slowly to the movers.

"Where do you want them lady." Asked one of the men, talking about the boxes they were holding in their hands.

"Actually, I would like if you would unload them in my car. It is in the back. Just bring your truck around and I will show you which car. Let me lock up and I will join you in the back."

The movers were able to squeeze every one of the boxes into her SUV. She was happy that James made her buy this vehicle last year for the store.

"It will be useful when you go antiquing for the store or when we go scuba diving for carrying all our gear and treasurers we find." He had said laughing aloud.

She had finally agreed but it had to be a Hybrid SUV, being self-conscious of environment.

When she arrived home, she drove her car as far as she possibly could towards the back yard to make it easier for her to unload the boxes on the veranda and then she would be able to transfer them in the house.

Detective Pondas did not show up that day at the store as he promised her, but he did show up at her house late that night.

At ten o'clock, she had just finish entering the last box and was relaxing sitting at the kitchen table when the doorbell rang, and she almost fell down of her chair. She slowly walked to the front door, pick up an umbrella standing by the corner, parted the curtain from the side window, and saw him. She unlocked the door and let him in.

"Detective Pondas, Allo! Nice of you to show up finally, I almost gave up on you. It is late and you are dressed in street clothes." She replied sarcastically.

He was wearing dark brown trousers with a beige polo shirt and a Brown jacket. He looked very handsome.

"Ms. Andrea, you are not the only case I have during the day. Should I say the death of your husband is not the only murder I have, since he was killed, two other murders happened no clues, no suspect?"

"So, you do believe its murder not just a hit and run?"

"A hit and run is a murder, Ms. Andrea, if the person does not stop and admit of doing it, and we later apprehend him or her, they are accused of murder."

"It is only semantics. You know what I mean."

"I am here now, what can I do for you?"

"I need answers, you need to catch this man, the one in a white car, which keeps following me and threatening my employee."

"Is that all?" He replied with a pad and pencil in hand pretending to write.

"No, that is not all!" Andrea added. "The man had a red baseball cap, covering half of his eyes. Does that sound familiar?"

"What do you mean?"

"This morning, I saw you with a man at the Hibiscus Restaurant, remember and what? The man had a red baseball cap. What were you doing with this man, his he a suspect?"

"Ms. Karr, if I choose to go for breakfast with someone it doesn't mean he is a suspect or under investigation and furthermore a lot of people sell red baseball caps and tourist love wearing them. You will see at least five to ten people every day wearing them."

"Sorry, everyone looks suspicious to me, just want to finish with this and continue with my life and return being happy again. Is that too much to ask?"

"No, can we sit down and maybe perhaps have a cup of coffee, please, if it is not too much to ask of you? We will be able to talk more quietly over coffee."

Detective Pondas walked on through to the kitchen, he was a tall man in is late thirties, well dress, good looking a severe cut on his face and deep black eyes. He had a dangerous look in his eyes. If he would not be an officer of the Law, she would probably be afraid of him. He might even be the kind of man that would drive a white car and run people over.

"Ms Karr, I have something to tell you that…might frighten you.

"What?"

"Mrs. Santos, we have found her on Virgin Gordo Island.

"Good, what did she say about her husband. Did she know about his death?"

"We found her in a room in Villa Key Hotel where she was murdered, by drugs to make it look like an overdose with a suicide note beside her bed."

"What did you just say? Mrs. Santos is dead, impossible, why would someone kill her? What make you say she was murdered not suicide?"

"Mrs. Santos had made flight reservation two days before to go see her dying mother in Canada. Her mother is a resident in a nursing home in the Laurentian Mountains and she had reserved a room in a hotel near by for a month. Someone with long-term plans does not commit suicide! I am sure the person who killed her did not know about her plans, in addition, the Santos yacht was anchored at the hotel marina. To my knowledge Mrs. Santos did not know how to navigate or dock a yacht."

He continued…

"To answer to your question: what was I doing with "that" man this morning. That man is a police officer, if you did not notice, the Restaurant has a marina, and he was delivering "The Santos" yacht to me for further investigation. This marina is the closes one to the police station; we rent docking spaces for police usage for special cases."

Andrea was sitting at the table sipping on her coffee without saying a word, confused and trying to make sense of what he was saying, she looked at him and…

"Detective Pondas, I really do not know what my husband or the Santos where up to. I believed James was working as a real estate sale person and on the odd time worked with the city for tourism. If he was doing something else, he really did a good job of keeping it a secret from me. "I… I…and she started crying uncontrollably.

"Please Andrea." This time he did not use Ms. in front of her name. He got up, went beside her, and touched her shoulder slightly.

"I have no doubt about you not being involved in what was going on, but your husband secret life put you in the middle of it and now you are in danger. You need to get a watch dog for your protection or even a hired bodyguard, it is expensive but if you can afford it, I really suggest you get one." He pleaded with her.

"Me! With a bodyguard that will follow me around like a little puppy. Are you serious? Is it that bad, they really think I know something? Why can I have just a police officer stopping by every hour? That should give me enough protection!"

"We cannot give you twenty-four-hour protection; the police force on the island is not that big and we do not have enough officers to cover that many hours and we would need to send someone at your store also. I am sorry but you will need to hire someone yourself if you want around the clock protection."

"You know I can not afford to pay someone 24 hours, but you said a dog, were can I buy a good guard dog, do you know places where they sell these trained dogs?" He asked.

"Yes, I know someone who works for the K-9 force. I am sure he can recommend a good breed of dog." He replied.

"K-9, you have that system here also?"

"We may be a small town by we do have modern administration and technology."

"I'm sorry I didn't mean anything by it." "Ok I will take the name of the person and I will call him."

"Good I will feel much better knowing you will not be alone here."

He turned toward the boxes at the far end of the kitchen. She had stacked them all neat against the wall going into the living room.

"What are those, may I ask?"

"Those are boxes belonging to James, I found them in the rented apartment he had in the city! If you wish you may look through them, you may find the answers to your questions, these are all about houses, condos and property lots James sold through 2005, 2006 and 2007, with also information on the Tourist guide industry and the address of the office which he was working from."

"Where did you find all of this?"

"Like I said before all of these came from James's apartment." He had another life beside the one he had with me. I really don't know who I married." She managed to say without crying.

He looked at her and knew not to pursue the matter further at this time. As they were finishing their coffee, the doorbell rang for the second time that night. Andrea jumps up and started shaking.

"It's ok, Andrea, I'm here, I will protect you, and he lifted his pant leg to reveal a gun in his boot. She looked at the gun and looked at him.

"Is this necessary? You are serious, aren't you?"

"Go answer the door I will be just beside you in the living room, if they try to hurt you or come in." He lifted the gun in the air.

"Oh! My God." As she wiped her forehead with the back of her hand.

"Just go answer the door please."

She slowly walked across the terra cotta, pushed the curtain just enough to reveal the outside steps for the second time tonight. She backed up to be closer to Pondas and said:

"There is no one there." She whispered.

"Look again, but be careful, do not open the door before you see who it is."

As she slowly pushed the curtain, the bell from the back door rang; she jumped and grabbed Pondas by the arm.

"Is that the front or back door?" He asked.

"It is the back door, what shall I do?"

"Go answer the door, but make sure you look who it is first."

"I am afraid…and she walked slowly back to the kitchen, she pulled the blind up a little and saw Puccino."

She opened the door slowly. "What do you want? It is late. What are you doing here?"

"May I come in? We need to talk!" As he pushed is way in.

"No, I told you it is late. Come back tomorrow."

"Let him in Andrea, I am curious to ear what Puccino has to say."

"Pondas old boy, what are you doing here so late, visiting the widow Karr?" He replied mockingly.

"Don't be so rude and you, what are you doing scaring Ms. Karr, by ringing the front door and then going around by the back door."

"I could say the same things for your old chap, what are you doing here, are you scaring Ms. Karr with your stories that someone is after her."

The two men were not friends, the tone of conversation was acid and the looks they exchange were icy. She was watching them going back and forth with threats and insults, scared of what could happen next.

"I came here on business, what about you, Puccino?"

"Same here, Ms. Karr is my client." Puccino replied with a smile.

"What do you mean she is your client?" He looked at Andrea with disappointing eyes.

"No, I am not." She screamed out at the man.

She turned towards the inspector and explained.

"He told me my husband was a client of is and now that James is dead, he says I am automatically his client, and I don't even know why my husband hired him." She tried to explain to Pondas. She turned towards Puccino. "Tell him it was James who hired you, tell him".

"Look Ms. Karr your husband asked me to do something for him and I did; now I want to be paid. That is all."

"But you never had a chance to tell him the result of your work, did you?"

"What?" Puccino replied.

"Yes, that's what you told me, you had scheduled a meeting with him when he was struck by the car, so, you never told him what you found out." She looked at the brown envelop he was holding in his hands

"Is that it?" She was pointing to the package. "Give me your report and I will pay you any amount you ask if I think it's worth it."

Pondas, looked at her and shifted is weight on the other foot to face Puccino.

"Are you sure you want it now, in front of Detective Pondas."

"Yes, I am sure, I don't know why my husband hired you and I am not responsible for my husband actions or anything else for that matter."

"Ok, as you please." He took her hand and placed the large brown envelope in it. "My bill is inside; you can pay me next time we see each other." Meanwhile still holding on to her hand, he saluted Pondas, slowly returned his attention to her and bends his head slightly raised her hand to his lips and kissed it. He looked up and smiled. "Darling." And left by the same door as he entered.

She screamed out at him. "Do not expect me to pay for this!" As she waved the brown envelop at him. "You can just take it back right now."

Andrea stood there holding the brown envelop in the air, has she watch him leave. She returned to the kitchen, drop the unopened envelop on the table, and saw the name printed on the envelop.

M. James Woods
C/o Ms. Andrea Karr
1563 St Marteen
Beef Island, Tortola, BVI

Pondas noticed Andrea's face changing color. He went over, took her hands in his and asked.

"What's wrong, are you alright?" Detective Pondas seemed genially concerned at this point.

She looked at him with tears in her eyes. "I am afraid to open it. It is strange that he addressed it c/o my name. It's like he was expecting something to go wrong or preparing to leave me." She looked at him. "Do you know what I mean?"

"Yes, believe it or not I know exactly what you mean." He replied. She looked at him, she could see in his eyes that he somewhat cared for her, and she found herself believing in him.

He slowly let go of her hands.

"I will leave you now, I don't think you are in any danger tonight, but please look into getting a dog for your protection and they are good company. If you need help in choosing one, let me know it will be a pleasure for me to accompany you."

"Oh! Certainly, thank you Detective Pondas. Good night."

Her mind was not really on dogs right now, it was more on the envelope she had left on the table.

"Thank you again, Detective Pondas. Good night."

He took a step and closed the gap between them, touched her shoulder and said very gently in her ear. "Get some sleep, tomorrow is another day, and it will be much better." He slowly traced the side of her face with his lips and kissed the corner of her mouth. Without a word, he left her standing there and walked towards the door without looking behind him. She rushed to the window and watched him drove off.

Chapter Four

Next morning she woke up early with the smell of coffee brewing, she sat up in bed, her heart beating fast trying to listen if someone was in the house, rubbing her eyes and pushing back her hair, she waited and started to laugh. She remembered she had set the coffee machine last night for six o'clock before going to bed. She took a quick shower; dress in a pair of white Capri and a bright orange T-Shirt, pull back her hair and walked towards the kitchen where the aroma of a good cup of coffee was waiting for her.

For the first time in two years, the shop stayed close on a Sunday. She decided that she needed a well-deserved day off and so did her employee Lana. The poor girl after all the verbal abuse she received the other day from the intruder, Andrea is lucky that the young girl still decided to come back to work for her.

A mug of coffee in her hand, pick up the brown envelop she had left on the kitchen table and walked out the back door, sat at the patio table trying to decide if she should open the envelop.

After she finished her coffee, she went inside to get herself another coffee with toast and jam this time. As she poured her coffee waiting for her toast to pop up, she saw through the kitchen window the famously brown envelop still not open on the patio table, trying to decide what to do. Suddenly a gust of wind lifted the envelop, carried it in the air, she let out a scream and started for the back door. She ran after it still twirling in the air, caught up to it just before it went over the water. Now that she had it in her hand again, should she destroy it by burning it in the BBQ pit or try to solve the mystery of James double life. She stood there looking at it and then heard the fire alarm in her house.

"Oh no! My breakfast" she ran back to the house, salvage what was left of her burnt toast with lots of jam. She poured herself another cup of coffee and returned outside.

An hour later she finally decided to rip the envelop open; she emptied the content on the picnic table. Inside she found several pictures of boats, old ships, wooden chests, and photos of beach with several sceneries.

She was surprised, she was certain it would have been pictures of girls partying or sunbathing nude or god knows what." She studied them carefully, one or two places she could recognized easily, it was the west point of Beef Island close to the airport and the other was at the end of her beach, the last picture was of two men standing beside a white car close to the sign of the Anegada Reef Hotel Marina. Included were also a map of the city and the surrounding waters of several islands. She returned to the picture of the two men, studied them carefully, she was unable to associate James with them, but one did look familiar, maybe he was once a client at her store?

She displayed everything side by side on the table and looked at it as an overall big picture, but nothing made sense to her. She gathered all the photos and inserted them back into the envelope and returned inside for her third cup of coffee still holding onto the envelop, on her way out she noticed the hammock in the corner of the veranda, and it looked so comfortable she decided on a small nap. After just a few sips of coffee she decided to close her eyes for a few minutes, she drifted away in oblivious, suddenly she was awakened by the noise of a car pulling in her driveway. She stayed there without moving as if she was paralyzed, then at the sound of her doorbell she got up, instead of going through the house to see who was at the front door she decided to walk around the outside of the house and greet her visitor. If she was careful, she could glance around the corner to view who it was in her driveway without being seen: There it was "the famous white car", her heart started beating faster and she could feel her blood pressure rising. When she raised her hand to wipe her forehead, she noticed she was still holding onto the envelop.

"What should I do, what should I do?" She mumbled to herself. She was trembling like a scare cat. She looked around to find a hiding place; she started to panic when she heard footsteps in the gravel walking toward her. She looked to the bushes beside the house, but they were too thin for her to hide in them, she faced the house and quickly decided to crawl under it. The crawl space was dark and damp and maybe with several geckos and snakes, but she had no choice, she wiggled herself underneath the house like a small animal and quickly moving when her visitor came around the corner. She held her breath at the site of a pair of brown trousers with crocodile boots passing by. The man had a noticeable limp on his right leg. He slowly walked around to the back, went up the stairs, and entered the house. She could hear him going from room to room-opening doors, closets, and drawers. He was looking for something, and then moved to the living room, Andrea could hear boxes being opened and then one by one drop on the floor, he moved to the kitchen, open the refrigerator door, she heard the sound of a can of pop being opened. He came back outside and stood on the back porch. He was probably looking around to see if he could spot her on the beach, he lit a cigarette and then pitched the can of pop on the ground, she almost screamed out when it hit one of the table legs, and the liquid came spitting out. He slowly descended the stairs, stops at the bottom, bent over to brush his pant leg full of pop and wiped his shoe. When she saw his jaw line she started shivering, she had to cover her mouth, scared she might let go a scream. He stood up and swore in Spanish and left the same way he came. She waited under the house for what seem to be more than ten minutes, she then carefully crawled out and ran inside and locked all the doors and windows. Still shaking of emotions, she dropped on her bed crying, she eventually stopped crying and fell asleep. Later that day the doorbell rang again, and she sat in her bed and waited to see if the person would leave or forced the door in. She waited without moving and then they rang the bell for a second time.

"What, not again?" she crawled out of bed and pushed the curtains of her bedroom window to see if it was someone she recognized. This time it was a gold Jeep in her parking lot. She ran to the front door and opened it with a force. "Hi, what are you doing her, what can I do for you?"

"Were you sleeping?" He asked.

"Yes, I was, sorry if I took a long time to answer the door, I thought you were the man in the white car again." She backed up and released the chain from the door.

"Sorry about scaring you like that and what do you mean you tough I was the man in the white car again?" He questioned her as he pushed his way in.

"I had a visitor this morning, but I didn't see who it was."

She could not tell him she was hiding under the house, she felt to embarrassed.

"Definitely we are going to get you a dog today."

"What? Right now, at this very moment? I am not prepared for a dog; I have no food or toys for it."

"I am off work today; I can go with you and give you advice and show you where to buy the best dog food at a discount price." He offered.

"Well!" At that moment, she notices he did not have his detective black suit on. He had a nice pair of clean blue jeans and a white golf shirt, closely shaved and sunglasses that made him look very attractive.

"Since you got all dressed up for me." She said teasingly. "I will go with you to buy me a dog. Give me a few minutes to change and I will be right with you."

He looked at her and smiled. "Take your time; I will wait for you outside on your patio, if that is Ok with you."

"Yes, that's fine. I have a pot of coffee on the stove, please help yourself. Cups are in the cupboard beside the stove, milk in the fridge."

He looked at the coffee and he whispered. "What year did you make this?"

"What? Were you talking to me?" She shouted.

"No! It's ok."

Before going outside, he noticed the boxes on floor with papers scattered and then he spotted the brown envelop on the kitchen table. He noticed it was opened and was tempted to look inside. What was so important that Puccino came over so late at night to talk to James's window about? He gave the envelope a push, hoping something would fall out, but nothing came out. He decided to leave it alone and ask Andrea about it. He went outside and sat the patio table. She came back outside fifteen minutes later in a pair of blue jeans and a light blue camisole. Her hair was pulled back in a twist with a Jaw claw.

"WOW! That did not take you long to get ready. You look good."

"Thank you. You didn't have any coffee?" She commented.

"No actually I like mine fresh. Did you have breakfast yet apart from the coffee?" He asked her.

"No, I had just coffee. Why you ask?"

"Before going to the dog farm, would you like to go for a bite to eat? It is a long drive in the country and by the time we get there it will be close to lunch hour!"

"What time is it?" As she glanced at her watch and noticed, she had overslept. "Ok, yes that would be nice. Let me put away these papers and we will be on our way."

"Andrea, may I ask a personal question?" What are these papers about?"

She looked at him, the envelop still clasp in her hand, pausing for a moment then decides to hand it over to him:

"Here! I have no idea what to do with this. I don't know what these papers or photos mean and I… have also boxes full of pictures if you ever want them, they are yours, also you will find Real Estate folders that maybe be helpful to you and the department, they could be holding evidence regarding James death and could clear his name."

"Are you sure you want to do this; it could also implicate him in different crimes or murders?"

"Yes, if these papers can help you clear James or…implicate him in any way to other murders then yes, its ok and it will probably help me forget him, and to clear my name of any doubts you may have. Please also take the boxes and destroy them after you are finish with them."

"Ok, if you do not mind, I will leave everything here for now, and maybe we can go through the papers together and try to figure them out."

"Ok, we can do that." she was puzzled why he would leave evidence lying around. He noticed she was surprised of his answer.

"Andrea, I will do everything I can to clear your name. Everything will be catalog. Don't worry about."

"Oh! I am not worried, I trust you will do the right thing, I would like the papers moved that is all. An intruder cane in my house and was prying through all my things, I am worried he may come back and look through the papers next time."

"You should move away from here; this place is too dangerous for you to be alone."

They gathered all the papers on the table and insert them back in the envelop and she showed him where the boxes of Real Estate information were and then to make her happy, they looked around the house for a secure place to store them.

Andrea suggested the pantry just of the kitchen. "It's big and with shelves." She informed the Detective and he agreed, they both decided when they return to store the papers.

Moments later they were leaving in his car, it was a gold-colored Jeep with brown stripes on the side, a large vehicle fully equipped and very comfortable.

They arrived at a small restaurant just of the ferry debarkation at Charlotte Amalie at the turn off highway 35.

After relaxing with a nice summer drink, Andrea felt very close to Pondas and was sharing life stories and private moments.

While sipping on her drink she realized:

"Officer Pondas, I do not know your name, I know your initials are T.P., but was does T., stand for." She questioned.

"T. stands for: The Officer Pondas". He looked at her and pulled down his sunglasses so she would not see the laughter in his eyes.

She gave him "Ah ah!" and pocked him in the ribs.

She looked at him and asked again. Officer what is your name?"

"My full name is Thomas J. Pondas."

"Thomas J. as in… what does J stand for?"

"Aren't you the investigator today? J. stands for…"

He stopped and took her by the hand and pulled it close to his mouth and said in a very soft voice while kissing her hand "James".

She pulled her hand from his grip, but he resisted and he did not let her go. "Don't Andrea; it's not my fault if my middle name is James. For your information, it is Detective Thomas J. Pondas as of today.

She looked at him and said: "Congratulations, are we ready, it's after twelve o'clock, let's go." She answered back with an icy cold voice.

They drove for an hour on the Highway 35 and turned into a dirt road for another 10 minutes before they got to this huge fence.

The inscription on the top of the archway said:

"Welcome to Gallows Bay Farm"

"What is "Gallows Bay Farm"?" She asked as she read it from a hanging shingle swinging from the overhead arch as they drove in through the gates. Between the trees far away, she could see buildings, more like barns and houses.

"This farm is a rehabilitation place for ex-prisoners and homeless people who have no where to go, due to bad luck, family abandonment, lost of business or home. Their choices are, instead of living on the street, we, a few members of the community, build this farm and made it a safe place for them to rehabilitate before attempting to go back into the society to find jobs."

"I didn't know about this place, and I have been living in St. Thomas for more than three years now."

"I am glad you didn't know most people in St. Thomas do not know about this place unless you were in prison or in trouble. This is a very private place to recuperate and get your life back in order with dignity."

The place was very well maintained, on the left a horse coral with a few horses roaming freely, dogs running all over the place and cows grassing in the next field.

"What a beautiful and peaceful place." She remarked.

Has the entered the parking lot behind the main house. On the far end was a large garage with three doors and one of them was open to reveal a white car like the one in the street at the time James was it.

"Why did you bring me here, I want to go. Who are you?" She screamed.

"What in hell is wrong with you, Andrea?"

"Don't tell me you don't see it? Over there, the white car."

"Andrea you will need to stop with this fixation of white cars. They are not all killers."

She took a deep breath and slowly climbs out of the Jeep. He joined her and took hold of her hand, she tried to resist but he pulled her toward him, she showed him she was not happy, but still she felt secure.

As soon as they reach the small garden surrounded by a fence, a pack of dogs rushed towards them, and she started to scream and back away.

"Don't tell me you are afraid of dogs. Are you?"

"No, but when there is a pack of dogs running towards me, I don't feel that brave." She replied hiding behind him.

In the distance came a whistling sound the dogs stopped in their tracks and an old man appeared from behind the barn.

"Thomas my boy, how are you." The man reached for Thomas's hand pulled him and then gave him a big hug.

Hi! Pop, how are you today."

"My arthritis is bothering me again; my feet are killing me and…" He glanced at Andrea. "That's about it, but, what about you Mr. Big Detective? Congratulations on your promotion son". As he gave Andrea a side wink.

"I am fine and thank you. Pop this is Ms. Andrea Karr, she needs a watch dog."

"Ms.… why would a beautiful lady like you need a watch dog, no man in your life?" The old man asked her directly.

"Thank you and no." Andrea replied shyly.

"Pop, Ms. Karr is a young widower; she lost her husband during Christmas time. Now let us talk about the litter of German Sheppard, remember about six months ago, the female that we breaded with Sam's father.

"Yes, and what about it?" He turned to face Thomas leaving Andrea to fend for herself with the dogs. At this point, they were all around her, liking and smelling her hands. One sniffed at her shoes, another her pant leg and one growled at her. She froze and the old man yield.

"Hey, stop that you crazy beast!"

"No, that is ok sir; it's my cat, they must be smelling her on my clothes." She answered back.

"Do you still have pups for sale from that litter?" continued Thomas without paying any attention to them.

He looked at her and replied. "Yes, that is the one." He was pointing to the dog beside Andrea.

"This one, I like him, he looks so vicious and yet gentle."

"He is not so gentle, Ms., if you try to hit Thomas or me, I am sure he would be happy to take your arm off and without thinking twice about it."

"What? Andrea backed a few steps away from the dog.

"No, Andrea do not be afraid of the dog!"

Thomas turned around and faced the old man. "Pop, what is the matter with you? I am trying to convince Ms. Karr to get a dog for her protection and you are scaring her off Pop, please she is trying to make a decision of getting a dog."

"No, that's ok Thom." Andrea replied and both men turned to face her when she pronounced his name.

"What? What did I say that was wrong?"

Detective Pondas smiled and replied. "No one ever called me Thom before that's all. It's always Thomas or law man."

"Oh!" She paused…" Is it alright if I call you Thom?"

"Yes, it is" replied the old man.

"Pop".

"It's been a long time since a woman called him Thom, and now, if you ask me, it's about time." He smiled at her.

"But no one is asking you." Replied Thomas and he continued showing Andrea several breeds of dogs, and she always came back to this small, male German Sheppard. He was very loving, and he enjoyed Andrea's hand petting and stroking him on his fluffy fur.

"This dog could be very well suited for you, Ms. He can also be very aggressive and dangerous as well as very playful and loyal to its master as you saw." The man was pointing out to her.

"I just love him. He is so beautiful. How much is he?" asked Andrea.

"Well, all my dogs are well trained, and this takes a long time and patience. On the other hand, he is not quite fully trained yet, so, for you dear, I would say five hundred dollars." He quickly informed her.

"Are you crazy, five hundred dollars?" Replied Detective Pondas.

"You will give her the dog since it's not fully trained. Do you understand me?"

"Thomas, tell me how you expect on making money if you keep giving away all of your dogs to the pretty women?"

"That is my business. Now when can she take the dog home?"

"I don't know you tell me, since it's your place?" Later the old man walked away, and all the dogs followed him.

"No, no don't go away, I want the dog." She started to run after the dog, finally caught up with him, was holding him on by the neck when the old man came back with a collar and a leach.

She looked at him and smiled. "Thank you, thank you so much."

"Don't thank me, thank the owner, Thomas."

"You're the owner of this big place?"

"No, I am part owner of this place with my father, but the owner of the littler and the parents of your dog" Supplied Pondas.

"He is your father? I thought when you were referring to him as Pop; it was in a figure of speech because he was old." She replied shyly.

"No, he is my dad and yes, he is old, stubborn and difficult at times, right old man?" Wink back at him.

They took the dog, placed it in the Jeep, and said their goodbyes to everyone that gathered around them when they toured the grounds.

As they were leaving the Ranch, Andrea could not help herself to ask.

"Thomas, may I ask a question?"

"Yes, what is it?"

"Is that your white car in the garage?"

He turned around faced her, lifted his sunglasses, and answered her with the most honesty. "Yes, it is."

She looked at him with discuss. For the rest of the trip back she did not say a word to him, she did not even look at the dog or pet it.

Arriving at her place, she jumps out of the Jeep, went straight for the door unlocked it and walked in.

James honked his horn, and she came back out standing in the doorway. "What?"

"You forgot your dog." He screamed at her.

"I…she looked at the dog and saw that beautiful face and couldn't tell him to keep it. She screamed out at the dog.

"Come boy, come…"

The dog looked at Thomas and he gave him a small shove.

"Go and take good care of her"

The dog jumps out of the Jeep, came beside Andrea, and licked her hand. She looked at Thomas, she tightens her lips together and waved goodbye and under her breath she let out a "Thank you." She closed the door and leaned against it and started crying, the dog looked at her and lay down beside at her feet. She listened for the sound of the Jeep leaving the driveway and then walked on through the kitchen with the dog following behind. She made herself a coffee and sat at the table looking out the back door watching the surf crashing on the beach wondering what to do next. Her concentration broke when she saw movement of people packing their chairs and mothers toweling down their children before guiding them towards the parking lot. She looked at the dog.

" Nothing is making sense what shall I do with all of this. Maybe Kelly was right about leaving this place and starting over back in Canada." The dog started barking; she looked at him and realized she did not have any food or toys for him to play with.

"Ok boy, we need to go out! Come with me, where going shopping, where did I place your leach?"

"Hi Charlotte, where have you been, I haven't seen you since yesterday!" The cat was purring and stretching in the hallway.

At the sound of Andrea's voice, the dog started running toward her, when the cat saw the dog, she rushed in the kitchen and through the cat door so fast and disappeared under the house.

"Buddy met Charlotte." She laughed.

She left the house around 6 o'clock with the dog to catch the 6:30 ferry for the inland. She arrived in the village of Charlotte Amalie and went straight for the overnight grocery store. She parked the car on the street before getting out she looked into the mirror and realized she had left without combing her hair or lipstick and her eyes were all red from crying before. She looked through her purse, found what she needed to make her self-presentable, roll up the car window just enough to give the dog fresh air and for him not to slip out.

"I will be right back. Stay." She gave the finger command to the dog just like Mr. Pondas showed her before she left, he obeyed and sat on the front seat and waited for her. The air was cooling down from the day's heat, but making double sure, he was not going to be too warm she parked car in the shade.

She was gone maybe less than ten minutes, when she came back out a police officer was writing her a ticket.

"Hey!" She screamed. "What are you doing? I am not breaking any law. I have money in the meter. What are you writing?"

"Ma'am, in Charlotte Amalie, it's against the law to leave an animal in the car without surveillance!"

"What? I just went in the store to get dog food. They do not allow pet in the store. What should I have done? Tell me." She stood in front of him with her hands on her hips.

"Ma'am I am just doing my job, if you have a complaint, go to the police station and file a complaint."

"I sure will. Thank you, who do I ask for?"

"Officer Pondas was the officer who enforced the animal cruelty law last year, now I am not sure who replaced him since he became Detective; Sorry Mrs…

"Andrea Karr… My name is Andrea Karr." She repeated.

"Mrs. Karr, I am not sure who you will be talking to, but you need to give him this ticket and he will listen to your explanation and decide if you are charged with cruelty."

"I didn't mistreat my dog. The window was open. OK." As she walked toward him. Thomas Pondas, I know the Detective, Thank you."

He handed her the ticket, she took it as she tried to hold on to the dog food and chew toys and with the other hand, she open the car door and climb behind the wheel. The dog was happy to see her and was licking her face and jumping on her as she tried to start the car.

When she arrived back at home, it was well over eight o'clock. She fed the dog and then played with him outside on the beach for an hour to tire him out. She places a blanket underneath the window in her bedroom for him with his squeaky toy and they both went to bed by ten o'clock. The dog looked at her and jumped on the bed. She would get show him back to his blanket to teach him to sleep on the floor but every few minutes the dog would jump back on the bed. After several times she looked at its beautiful face and decided the dog would sleep in her bed.

Chapter Five

Next morning, she was, waken by a wet tongue liking her face. She opens her eyes slowly and she wiped her face:

"Hello! Boy. Did you have a good sleep? What is wrong, need to go outside, come on boy? She looked at the dog waging his tail and being exited.

"Come boy. Well, today I need to find you a name; I can't always call you boy all the time." The dog just sat their and looked at her.

She did her morning ritual, house cleaning with the dog following her everywhere, walk the dog, feed him and the cat, empty the litter box. She realized she would do this every morning before leaving for work and upon her return every night. She looked at him and wondered what she got herself into. Before they got married, they had decided not to have children.

"Why did I just buy dead bolt locks for the doors instead of you?" She smiled at him and shook her head slowly at him.

For the first morning, she managed to do every thing and was out of the door at eight o'clock sharp. She got her coffee bagel and her newspapers the same as she did every Monday morning. However, this morning was different; she was holding a leach with a very agitated dog. She could not leave the dog alone at home with Charlotte, so she decided to bring him instead of her cat. She opened the store, everything was going great, she sent Lana for breakfast and more coffee for her, she brought dog food and a bowl for water. She placed the bowls close to the back door. Everything was going well; her emails were all answered and then the door opened, and she looked up to see who it was…it was him!

"Why his he back here this morning?" She whispered.

Detective Pondas was standing at the door, without entering.

"Good morning Ms. Karr!" He replied coldly.

She returned his salutation with the same coldness. "Good morning, Detective."

"Hello Buddy."

"What? What did you just call me?" She snapped back at him.

"Don't get mad, I was talking to the dog. I named him Buddy when he was born." He replied has he bent down to pat the dog and kiss his nose.

"Sorry I was sure you were being smart ass with me. Buddy you said. I love it; it is a good name for him. I was looking for a name this morning that would fit him with his beautiful face and brown eyes. I could not find a name that I like and would suit him. Thank you, I will continue calling him Buddy, and it goes well with Charlotte my cat. Looking at the dog's response when you said hello to him, he seems to like it also."

She patted the dog's head. "Hey! Buddy." She then returned her attention to the Detective. "What can I do for you, Detective Pondas?"

"Please Andrea, can we forget what happen yesterday and just continue from there, I do not want to go back to Detective Pondas and Ms. Karr please."

"And where was that?" She replied has she picked up her coffee cup from the table, he tried to block her passage to look into her eyes for sign of passion or feelings, but her eyes showed him she did not.

He moved to let her pass. "Never mind I guess I was mistaken. I will have information on your late husband's case within a week. Goodbye." Lana came in while he was still holding the door and he saluted her and in return, she smiled back at him.

"Is everything ok, Ms. Karr?"

"Everything is just dandy.' She replied sarcastically.

During the rest of the week, the young girl was doing a great job in the store and there was no more encounter with the person in the red cap, the white car, or the Detective. They both were very busy preparing the store for the Spring Fiesta in a few weeks. Friday would be here in a few days, and she felt that a well deserve day off was appropriate. She would call Lana on Friday morning to advise her she would be away all day and if any problems, she could be reached at home or on her cellular phone and she would give her two-day weekend.

Friday finally arrived, she made the call to Lana, everything was all right, and she had no problem with her being alone for the day and having two days off.

Andrea showered, packed a light lunch for her and water and kibbles for the dog she also packed food for Charlotte just in case she decided to show up. She would see her and leave food for her every morning, but she did not want to stay in the house when the dog was in.

Instead of taking the car and drive at the end of the beach, she decided to walk all the way. She was looking forward to a full day out just relaxing and playing with the dog. It is a long walk, but it is worth it. She will need to bring a blanket and the small cooler, the last time she ventured at the other end she was with James, and he carried most of the gear, will she be able to carry all of this by herself. She was so much looking forward to a good swim, lazing around under a loblolly tree and reading a good book or just do nothing all day. These preparations for her special R&R Day brought back memories. Will she even trust a man again and capture what she had with James, the love of her life, he couldn't even be honest with her. What about all the other men are all like that?

She arrived at the end of the beach a few minutes past ten. She organized all her belongings by placing the cooler against a tree, she laid the blanket close by making sure only part was in the sun, dog toys and water near the cooler.

"Just enough sun and just enough shade, right Buddy." The dog seems to understand what she was saying and dropped on the blanket beside Andrea. It was truly a beautiful day, a few clouds moving in the sky but not near enough to disturb their sunshine. She removed her sandals and her jeans revealing a skimpy orange bikini bottom. She hesitated to take her T-Shirt off because of the hot burning sun on her shoulders and then decided:

"Well just for a swim and then I will put it back on." She was explaining to the dog has if he new what she was talking about. She ran in the water splashing and giggling, the dog followed her close behind.

"Buddy, do you love water? Come boy, play with me."

They splash, ran and swam for an hour or more, after the two of them were terribly tired they both fell on the blanket and closed their eyes for what seamed for a few minutes but actually, when she woke up a little more than an hour had passed.

Andrea sat up, rubbing her eyes looking around for her dog Buddy; at first sight, she could not see him. She stood up started walking towards the other end of the beach; maybe he found is way back home, but no dog. She started back to where she had placed the blanket and started to shout his name.

She knew there was no one else on the beach at this time of day, so the dog did not follow a child or an adult. She called his name several times and no responses. She looked in the water, up and down the beach, under the trees, behind big rocks or sand dunes, nothing.

It was now close to six o'clock several hours has passed and the sun was setting slowly behind the mountain in the west. She was very worried of what could have happened to her dog. The visibility was getting much better the sun was no longer in her eyes and the bright reflection in the water was almost all gone. Her eyes were able to focus better on a distance and running back to the blanket she notices the sunrays bouncing of a shiny object in the mountain. She decides to investigate, thinking the dog might have notice it and went to explore.

As she was approaching, she could hear a faint noise, more like a muffled moaned. As she came closer, she realized what it was and started running towards the cry in her bare feet. She climbed the mountain pushing away branches and screaming Buddy's name at the same time.

"Buddy, Buddy come here boy." Every time she screamed the dog's name, the noise sounded like an animal in pain. As she was getting closer, she felt sick to her stomach just the though of what she might find. Finally, she saw him: Buddy was tied up tight to a tree and a red scarf around his nose. The dog was slightly dehydrated and at the sight of Andrea, he became agitated. Andrea trying to get him free, but the dog was moving and crying so much that the rope became tighter and tighter and was hurting the dogs neck.

"Buddy, what happened? Who did this to you?" Kissing his nose and talking to him calmly as Andrea tog on the rope to finally releasing the dog. When she freed the dog, she heard a noise in the bushes below. She held on to the dog by the collar and walked him to a safer place. She waited without moving, as it could be his attacker returning. She sat on the ground trying to focus on what was running in the bushes, she got a glimpse of a man with camouflage clothing and a red baseball cap running down the hill. Her heart skipped a beat; she held the dog on tight and started shaking.

Buddy was trying to console Andrea by licking her face and yapping. "Buddy, shut up." She closed her eyes to hear more clearly and suddenly the sound stop. She immediately opened her eyes and quickly looked around her.

"Dead silence". She whispered. "Sorry Buddy, I shouldn't say words like dead at the present time and she kissed the dog's nose."

She got up, looked through the branches and in the distance, she saw a man running on the beach going towards her blanket. She watched and observed him very carefully. She tell him drop something on her blanket. She waited a few minutes and started her descended from the mountain with Buddy limping beside her. She tried to pick him up, but the dog was too heavy for her.

"Come on boy; be brave, so much for a peaceful day at the beach Yeah!"

The dog followed her closely beside her leg.

When she reached the beach, she pulled Buddy in the water; she squatted down in the water and with her, both hands she made the form of a small bowl and gave him water to drink. He drank several hands full, she washed his face, nudged him to lie down in the water to cool him off. She brushed the mud from his fur, reassured him everything was going to be okay with hugs and kisses on his forehead while at the same time keeping a vigil eye of their surroundings. They returned to the blanket as sat there for the longest time without moving. She remembered the mysterious man dropped an object on the blanket; she noticed a piece of paper underneath Bud's front paw.

"Push over Bud." Has she gently pushed his paw.

She could see handwriting on it. She unfolded the crimpled paper and red the note:

"Next time you or the dog won't be so lucky."

She looked around one more time and could not see anyone, but she could hear the noise of a car driving away. She packed everything up, took Buddy by the collar and walked her way back home. As she got closer, she could feel eyes on her and Buddy was getting more agitated than before. When she arrived at the house, she immediately picks up her car keys and drove directly to the farm to see Thomas father.

Arriving at the farm, she noticed the white car was still in the open garage. As she parked her car, the dog jumped out and went directly to the old man walking up to her, she noticed he was not alone; several men were near a broken fence looking at her. One of them started running towards the bunkhouse when she looked at them.

"Buddy, what happen to you?" The old man gave a nasty look at Andrea.

"Hi! I need your help. The dog was abducted this afternoon."

"What did you say? The dog was abducted, how?" Questioned the worried old man.

"We were at the beach having fun and we both fell asleep on a blanket, and when I woke up the dog was gone. It took me more than two hours to find him and when I did, he was tided up to a tree and a red scarf over his nose to prevent him from barking."

She pulled the scarf from her pocket, showed it to him, and then returned it to her pocket.

"He had mud all over him as if he was drag up the mountain or maybe he gave a struggle and was pushed on the ground." Andrea with tears in her eyes tried to explain.

"Don't worry I will examine him and if he needs medical attention I will call my friend Peter, he is a veterinarian, he lives down the road." He assured Andrea.

"Ms..."

"Please call me Andrea."

"Andrea, can I see the red scarf again.

"Yes, why do you know who owns such a scarf?" She questioned.

"Well, I am not sure, but I did see a similar scarf here a few months ago when a young lad stayed with us and a gang of hoodlums paid him a visit for a few days. Thomas had to use force to kick them out of the property. They were always picking fits with the others." He noticed Andrea was looking at him with big eyes.

"Thomas did mention to you what this farm stands for, right?"

"Yes, he did mention something to that effect. Why would they be after me, I have nothing they want and poor Buddy, he just arrived at my place. I am afraid he won't want to come back home with me."

"Don't worry about it, he seems to love you. You didn't hear him bark or struggle beside you at all."

"No, like I said, we played so much in the water that both of us were tired, we just fell asleep on the blanket, as the same time she was scratching the back of her neck.

"Bring him around back, I will check him out." As he observed her scratching away. "Are you ok?"

"Yes, I think so, thank you."

The man left with the dog and came back an hour later. "You are sure you didn't hear or saw anyone on the beach close by."

"No, there was no one. The beach was deserted as usually this time of year."

He looked at her and said: "He was poison by what looks like a dart, so they must have used a dart gun from not to far away. And it would explained why he never barked; he probably didn't even ear them approaching."

"What he was poison, poor baby, can I see him." Andrea entered the room and saw Buddy sitting on top of a huge table, she approached him and kissed the top of his head and then hugged him. The dog responded by wagging its tail.

"That means they were beside me, how come I did not wake up. I should have felt someone close by."

"Andrea, he will be alright just don't let him outside alone for a couple of days; he will be a little drossy for a day or so but nothing to worry about. Give him plenty of water not too much food, his stomach may react to the poison."

"Ok I will take good care of him. Thank you very much."

"Does Thomas know about this incident?"

"No. Please don't tell him, not just yet anyway." She pleaded.

"He may think I can't handle a dog."

She started to walk toward her car; she turned around and faces the old man.

Oh! May I call you Pop? She asked.

"Yes, that's what my friends call me." And he winked at her.

"May I ask you something…the white car in the garage, it belongs to Thomas, is that correct?"

"Yes, that stupid car, it's an obsession with him, he as been trying to fix it up. It will probably never run again, but it does keep him busy, ever since his wife died in 1998 in a car crash."

"I didn't know he was married before. And you say the car doesn't run?"

"No, it doesn't. I just said, they had a car accident with it, she died at the scene of the crash, and he has been trying to rebuild it ever since. Why are you so interest in his car?"

"Well, you see my husband was struck by a white car just like that one and he died also at the scene of the accident, but I was a hit and run. I kind of accused Thomas indirectly that I had a suspicious that he was part of it."

"Thomas, he is an officer of the Law he doesn't not go around killing people for nothing."

"Well, it does happen…some cops do turn bad for the right amount of money, but I am not saying Thomas is a bad cop, but I have a lot of unsolved questions."

"Everybody does. Ms., I like you but if you continue talking like that, I will ask you to leave and not come back here again."

The old man turns towards the barn and starts walking away." What are you doing now?" He screamed at the man sitting inside the barn door and looking at Andrea.

Andrea did not notice what the old man was looking at and continued talking.

"No, I am sorry; I didn't mean that Thomas killed my husband I know he didn't. I said it is a car like that one. That's all."

After explaining herself repeatedly and telling the story about her husband James, it was now well past super time and she was dirty and tired from her long day, she left with Buddy who was feeling much better.

Just has she started crossing the farm gate, she saw it, the Gold Jeep coming up the road straight for her.

"Should I stop and talk to him or should I just drive on. Buddy what should I do?"

Too late he stops beside the road to let her pass, she did not have a choice now but to talk to him. She slowed down just enough to say:

"Hi! Thomas, bye Thomas while scratching the back of her neck like crazy" And wave goodbye at him.

"Wait." He screamed but to no avail, she just continued.

Furious with her he continued to the farm where he questioned his dad into revealing what she was doing there.

"Why, what did she want, how long did she stay?" Questioned Thomas.

"Sons slow down, someone would think you were interested in the lady."

"I am but not in that way, she is in danger for her life and also the principal suspect in one of the cases I am working on."

"Oh! You mean the death of her husband. You do not think that she killed him, do you?"

"No, and how do you know about her husband?"

"She told me what happen to him, and I believe her she didn't kill him."

"So do I but, why he was killed, that is another story if I believe it or not. She might know more than she is letting on. Pop's you still didn't tell me why she came to see you?"

"Oh! Yes, Buddy was abducted, and she wanted to make sure everything was ok with him.

"What! Abducted, when, by whom?" Thomas screamed out at the old man more worried about the dog safety than Andrea.

"That, she didn't know!"

"What do you mean, she didn't know? Where was she when this happened?"

"She was sleeping beside him when it happened."

"She was what? Come on Pop, you are not making any sense, what did she say?"

After the old man tried to explain to his son what happened he walked away. "Thomas where do you think you are going, what about your chores, it's your turn today?"

"I decided I am going to visit Andrea and see for myself if the dog is ok, if I am not satisfied with her answers I will be right back with the dog."

"Andrea was also pretty much shaking up; maybe you should ask her how she feels.

"Why?"

"I think she may have been drugged also."

"Goodbye Pop" And he speed out of the driveway.

Arriving at the corner of Andrea's Street, he was passed by a speeding white car going towards the other way. He accelerated and reached the lane way and saw a police patrol car in her drive way. Immediately he rushed inside the house without even knocking and was surprised to see an officer and Andrea sitting at the kitchen table, talking.

"What's going on?" Asked Thomas worried.

"Sir, I was just taking a report about someone who mistreated her dog Buddy." At the same time, the officer stood up when he recognized the Detective.

The dog stood up at the sound of his name and came running in the kitchen. He looked at everyone, ran beside Andrea, and sat at her feet. Andrea petted the dog and gave him a treat that was lying on the table.

"Andrea what is going on? What happen to Buddy? Who mistreated him, are you ok? Were you hurt, my father said you were scratching a lot behind your neck?"

"Thomas"

He stopped at the sound of her voice calling him by his name.

"Thomas, I am ok and so is Buddy. Your father checked him out and he was poison with a dart gun and tied to a tree on the mountain."

"What mountain, there is no mountain around here?" He was getting impatient with the information not coming fast enough for him.

"I will start over my story." As she glanced to the officer. "If you don't mind officer?" The officer waved back ok at her.

Andrea started: "Buddy and I went to the end of the beach for the day."

"What beach?" He interrupted her.

"This beach, Long Bay Beach, at the other end of the island and we played in the water for hours and then we both fell asleep on a blanket under a loblolly tree. When I woke up…"

"What? What happened when you woke up, Andrea?" Insisted Thomas.

"Please, let me continue…When I woke up, Buddy was gone, I looked for him everywhere, in the water, near the car in the parking lot, in the bushes, I couldn't find him, and then, there was a flash of light in the mountain. Ah!" She exclaims. "Now I understand why the flash of light, someone had probably reflected light on a mirror in my direction for me to find Buddy, because at that moment, when I saw the light, I knew buddy would have also investigate the source of the light just like I did. When I arrived at the spot, Buddy was tied up and gag with a red scarf, kind of a bandana, he was weak and that is why I brought him to your father for a check up, I was worried." Andrea took a long breath and looked at Thomas.

"And that, is what happen, do you think you will be able to find who did this?" She turned towards the officer.

" Yes, we will." Replied Thomas before the officer could himself reply.

"We will do our best Ma'am."

"Officer, I will take care of this case, I am sure it's all related to the case I am working on now." Replied Thomas.

"Oh! I also have a note from the kidnappers." She let you and rushed to the laundry room where she had placed the blanket and towels.

"What, they left a note?" Thomas looked at the officer.

"Sorry Sir, I didn't know, this is the first I ear about it." He informed him.

"Thomas I just remembered, don't get on his case, he didn't know. I placed the not in my beach bag with the towels and I forgot about it."

When she returned in the kitchen, she had a piece of crumple paper. She handed it over to the officer; he looked at it and then handed it over to Thomas and wrote note in his black book.

"Next time you or the dog won't be so lucky." Thomas red the note aloud as he looked at Andrea.

"Are you going to take this seriously now, these people are not playing around. You need to be more careful."

"But I was." Explain Andrea. "I even went to the end of the Island to pass a quiet day alone with Buddy." She replied while scratching the back of her neck.

"Andrea, did you also examine your arms and legs for small puncture wounds."

"What on me no, but, I do have this bite on the back of my neck, it is very itchy."

"Let me see." He slowly lifted her hair; slowly and carefully examine the base of her neck. He traced his finger all around the base of her neckline. She could feel the electricity that he was transferring to her, she felt warm, and she started shaking.

"Are you alright Andrea, you are shaking, my dad said you may have a kind of reaction if you were also drugged."

However, what he did not know is the reaction was due to his closeness of his body and the way he was touching her with his fingers.

"What is this? Officer, come here please! Does this look more like a puncture wound or an insect bite."

She started to move away. "What? You think I was also drugged?"

He pulled her back towards him and exposed the base of her neck to the officer. He examined it carefully and said. "Sir it is a puncture wound probably made by a dart." He replied with a professional tone.

"Thank you, officer. Andrea, you live alone on a half deserted island, you go around sleeping on a deserted beach, exposing your self to who ever is watching you. You never know your every move could be film and they may be waiting for the right moment, like today, to…"

"To what? Kill me! For what?"

"Andrea, I need to talk to you about James. He looked at her and continued slowly. He was involved in different… how can I say this without hurting you?"

"Thomas please just say it; I don't care anymore about James. With everything that is going on in life right now if he is responsible, I want to know about it. I will never forgive him for what he is putting me through, I feel no more love towards him."

"Ok, here goes…Remember the deed that was left on…Mr. Santos body?"

"Yes."

"Well, the deed was made to your name remember and it also contained the exact location of three other lots on Beef Island, and apparently you also own a diving boat with the most expansive diving gear docked at the Anegada Hotel Marina beside the Santos boat and a few apartments and condos.

"What, you must be mistaken, are you sure I owned all of that. Believe me I did not know?

"Well, you do own all of that and maybe more we are not finish investigating." He continued. "James transferred everything to you personally, he made sure in case he was arrested you would keep the lot."

"What is going to happen now?"

"The investigation is not over, far from it and you will probably be indicted."

"What indicted, why? I have nothing to do with this and I will say it again and again until you all believe me. What will happen to me, my reputation? If this goes public, I will be bankrupt, no one will want to work for me or supply me with merchandises."

"An indictment can be sealed so that it stays non-public until it is unsealed."

"What can unseal it? She asked all worried. "Can I go to jail?"

"It may be unsealed, once the named person, YOU, is arrested or has been notified by police."

"Who decides to seal or unseal the indictment?"

"The prosecutor often has a choice to indict from a grand jury or filing a document directly with the court."

"Damn you James, honestly I would kill you if you were not already dead!" Andrea took her head between her two hands and started to cry. The two men looked at each other without saying a word and waited. After she wiped her tears with the back of her hand, she continued. "I was not part of this charade honestly, what am I going to do?"

The officer looked at her and then at Pondas. "We will help you clear your name Ms. Andrea."

"We? What do you mean, we? This is and investigation murder case it's no longer a police matter."

"Ye… es, I know that, but I am offering my services free of charge to Ms. Andrea because I am certain she is not guilty and telling us the truth."

"You are, are you? Well, I guess we will need all the help we can get to catch these murderers."

"These, you mean there is more than one, and you two are willing to believe me that I am innocent?"

"We need to find you a good lawyer because any day now you will be indicted. Listen." He took a folded page from inside his black book and started reading from it.

"Where is it? …bla…blabla. Ok this is it, listen. {Some indictment for complex crimes especially those involving conspiracy or numerous counts of murder, he or she will be held over for a preliminary hearing. If the judge determines that there is sufficient evidence to believe that the defendant committed the crime, it is said that the defendant is held to answer.}"

"And all of this means what? I can go to jail, is that it?"

"Yes, maybe for six months or more until the trial starts."

"Six months, I would lose everything, my store, my house, my car, everything."

"And your properties, your yacht, your condo…!" The officer stopped talking when he noticed her face changing color.

"I don't have a boat or properties." Scream Andrea tight lip at the officer.

"But yes, you do Andrea, no matter what you say, you do have all of those things." Thomas tried to explain to her.

"Tomorrow we will go retrieve your boat from the hotel Marina on the Anegada Island and then we will visit your properties on your island. You said you and James used to go pass time at the beach. Did you go often or just once or twice?"

"Actually, we went often especially for picnics, at least twice a month. We would pass the entire day, swimming, playing making l……" she blushed and continued…We were making plans for our future, we were going to build our dream house at the end of the bay."

Thomas said slowly. "Did you always go alone or would you invite friends sometimes to join you."

"We always went alone but never stayed alone, there was always someone stopping by in their boat and talk with James for a few minutes or drop papers for him or envelops. He always replied they were satisfied customers dropping to say hello and thanking him. I immediately assumed they were Real Estate customers."

"They would just talk and then leave?" Pondas wrote a few words in his little black book and returned his attention back to Andrea.

"And then what?"

"Usually afterwards he would go for a walk alone and disappear in the bushes at the further end of the beach… just about a few feet where I found Bud. I never asked him why he was going there. I assume he was going to…" She looked at the other office softly said, "….to the bathroom. Wow, I sure feel stupid now. What was he doing out there?" she said in a low voice as she walked away ashamed of her husband trickeries.

"Well tomorrow we will know more." She twirled around on her toes and looked at them. "What? What do you mean we will know more?"

"Yes, because in the early morning we will go investigate."

"Are we going to Anegada to retrieve the boat also?"

"Yes, Officer Elfino will boat us to Anegada Island, and we will come back with your boat and make a stop at the end of your beach and go over inch by inch the ground where you found Buddy and afterwards return back the boat at the police Marina and pick our cars at the end of the day."

"Yes, but Detective Pondas, being in the boat will that not compromise the investigation?" Question the officer.

"We will process the boat at Anegada once finished we will return with the boat, no compromising evidence or scene, I will make sure of it."

"Ok, what time should we leave tomorrow? She curiously asked.

"Let's all meet at the Restaurant at six o'clock tomorrow morning, have a good breakfast and start on our way around seven. We should get there by nine thirty and on our way back by noon. Arriving at Long Beach by one thirty… all of this ok with you Andrea?"

"Let see! Six, seven, noon, one, back here, sure, no problem, but I will be bringing the dog with me."

"That's ok, you should bring him with you, he should accompany you every where you go, that is why I got you the dog. I will bring Brutus, my dog; they will keep each other company. My dog is always with me on my days off and when I am at the farm, he loves it there.

Chapter Six

That evening sleep did not come easy to Andrea, she tosses and turn all night and so did Buddy. When five o'clock came around, she was startled by the sound of the alarm clock; they both had just drifted into a light sleep startled. She immediately got up, showed, dress in a light pair of beige short and matching sleeveless shirt. She prepared her sneakers, bathing suit, towel, sweater and a sun hat, now she had to find something to carry them, she found her overnight bag that James gave her last Christmas, it was perfect just big enough for what she wanted to brings. She also remembered to pack food, bowl and water for Buddy and his favorite toy. She applied sunscreen and lipstick, brush her hair and tie up it with hairclip in the back; she was out the door in exactly twenty-eight minutes, a record time for her.

She arrived at the Hibiscus Restaurant at exactly five past six o'clock. She had to break a few speeding rules to get there on time and she did. She parked her car and noticed Thomas was already on the dock loading a boat. She grabbed Buddy by the collar and her bag and started for the pear. Thomas saw her immediately and came to her rescue her from Buddy's agitated state about the narrow path they were walking on to get to the boat.

"Good morning!" He saluted her with a big smile has he grab her bag and stroke Bud on top of his head.

"Good morning! I am not sure it is a good one, I will let you know after my second cup of coffee." She replied with a yawning gesture.

"What? Is six o'clock to early for you? I am up since four thirty. It was a beautiful sunrise this morning" we will have a great sunny day today."

"I haven't had my coffee yet, so don't tell me what king of day it is going to be I will decide after breakfast."

He laughed. "Not a morning person, are you?" He dropped all the bags in the boat, took her by the hand and guided her up the ramp to the restaurant.

"Come. Let's put some coffee in you before you fade away, also a good hearty breakfast will do you no harm". As he looked up and down at her perfect skinny body.

Andrea had lost more than a few pounds since the death of her husband; she did not mind because she was happy with her appearance.

"Come, Officer Banji is already here waiting for us."

"Officer who?"

"Officer Banji! He will be replacing Officer Elfino."

"Why? I like him."

"He has been transferred to another case at the other end of the island. Officer Banji is quite capable of working with us on your case and he is familiar with the Santos."

They walked up the ramp with Buddy and met with Officer Banji and Buster in the restaurant. Andrea liked him right away. She admires is demure attitude and his politeness. He was about her age and beautiful light tan skin for an islander. They had a good hearty breakfast and were on their way no later than seven o'clock.

The trip went smoothly, the dogs mostly slept all the way and upon arriving at the Hotel Marina, Andrea grab Buddy by the collar and Buster followed behind while the two men grabbed all the other bags. Thomas right away noticed two men looking at a yacht at the other end and signaled Officer Banji by a hand signal: when the men noticed the officer and Pondas they started to run and jump in a speed boat parked on the opposite side and rod off. Detective Pondas who was behind Andrea signal Banji not to say a word to Andrea.

She was busy with the two dogs therefore she did not notice a thing. They started walking along the docks and came to a stop beside the yacht where the two men were lurking. The name of the yacht was. J&A Forever.

"I would guess this is your yacht, Andrea." As he turns towards her.

Her mouth dropped open and her eyes could not get any wider as she gawks at the biggest yacht in the small marina.

"No…this can't be James?"

"Well according to the papers I have here, it says: Yacht…White with navy blue strips, license number 345234 named J&A Forever. See." He was pointing to the name below the description of the yacht.

In addition, he continued… "Owner: Ms. Andrea Karr 1563 St. Marteen Beef Island, Long Bay Beach. Tortola. BVI."

"Wow! That is all she could come up with and stood there with her hands over her mouth.

Thomas heard a noise, jumped inside the vessel, and signaled the officer to come on board and to follow him: They both drew their gun and Andrea panic.

"What, what are you doing." She screamed.

"It's just precaution, don't worry about it."

Officer Banji went forward, gave a quick look around and ten minutes later, and gave the two thumbs up for boarding. Thomas went forward entered the cockpit and had a look around, moving to the helm area he looked at the panel board with all the instruments and notice the gasoline gage was full.

They were now ready to bring the vessel back to Charlotte Amalie marina.

This yacht was a luxurious vessel of forty-five feet long. Having entered by the extra-large extended swim platform, Andrea was able to see the entire boat and its splendor. She ventured inside the boat with the two dogs; first, she saw a small lounge with a bar and a small refrigerator complete with an icemaker and plenty of cupboards to store refreshments. The dogs went forward, and Andrea followed them. They stop at the top of three curved stairs that took her below deck. Below there was a queen size bed and two set of drawers on each side. She opens each drawer and finds only a few things that could have been James personal belongings, a pair of socks, a tie and swim trunks, a wardrobe at the back, contain a shirt, pants and a blue blazer.

She returned up the stairs where Thomas was exploring the other end of the yacht. A small dining table with six chairs especially made to slide easily under the table giving the room more space, a small galley was beside and well appointed. It included refrigerator/freezer, microwave/convection oven set into the cabinetry below the counter and a large double stainless sink. There was a built-in coffee maker, electric stovetop, and more cabinets. Everywhere there was full standing headroom, also a full bathroom with shower separated from the sink and toilet.

"How could he afford this? What was he doing with this yacht?"

"I have an idea, but I am sure you don't want to know right now."

Andrea looked at him, stared for a minute, she turns, and walked away just before tears started rolling down her cheeks.

He continued his search for incriminating evidence with paying any attention to her for the next ten minutes.

"There are a lot of special options that must have come handy."

"Like what?" She raised her voice for him to hear her.

"Like a big engine and hydraulics."

After going over the entire boat, checking for anything unusual, Thomas gave an order to the officer.

"Officer Banji would you investigate the prop and anchor, make sure they are secure or if we are carrying anything unwanted attachment to the Yacht"

Officer Banji obeyed Thomas and came back a few minutes later without his shirt or pants, wearing a bathing suit and all wet.

"Everything looks ok, Sir."

Thomas ordered Andrea to sit down until the completion of the inspection was concluded.

"What kind of clues are you looking for?" She asked Pondas.

"What James was doing with this boat?" He replied without looking at her and continuing opening every drawer and cupboard.

The two men thoroughly inspected every little detail.

An hour later, Andrea saw Thomas instruct the officer to return to the police station with a plastic bag and verify if anyone had called to know the whereabouts of Mrs. Santanos or of Ms. Andrea and to meet them back at Andrea's home later that evening.

Thomas and Andrea said their goodbyes to the officer and they left their separate ways: Officer Banji went south and Andrea and the Detective went west. One hour in their voyage everything was going well, they were enjoying each other company and the dogs were lying motionless due to the movement of the wave. Thomas noticed the East sky covering with big rolling grey clouds moving faster than normal. He decided to radio in for the weather forecast. He talked for several minutes in French Creole afterwards in Spanish and finally finished with English and what she heard made her nervous: "We will try to make it to Long Bay Beach at Beef Island before it hits. She believed the man at the other end of the transmission replied it was too dangerous and they should not take the risk. Thomas replied they had enough time to make it due to the size of the yacht.

"We will take our chances, thank you over and out."

"Take our chances before what hits?" Questioned Andrea worried.

"Nothing to worry about, a tropical storm is approaching the Virgin Islands. The storm force winds could reach 37 to 74 miles per hour in the next 36 hours. It could get pretty ugly, and they advise everyone to get off the water as soon as possible."

She looked at him and turned on her heals towards the black sky. "But hurricane season is finished. We are in late December."

"Well, that is why Anegada island has so many shipwrecks stories, they all happen in unexpected storms."

"How far away are we from Beef Island?" She moved closer to him.

"It's more than fifty minutes from here, that way." He was pointing towards the West.

"And in which directions is the hurricane coming from?" She asked.

"It's in that direction," he was pointing south. "Southwest going towards Puerto Rico, but it as been known a hurricane will turn and go the opposite way."

"So, we should be ok since we just left from Anegada? However, Officer Banji is going in that direction, exact?" Asked Andrea worried.

"To answer your first question, I saw Hurricane's Coming from the North going towards Northeast and ten miles before hitting the shore it makes a complete 360 degree to Northwest." He looked all around and studied the clouds, and for Officer Banji, he will make it on time, do not worry about him, Coast Guards are meeting him halfway due to the size of his boat, they do not want him to take any chances.

"I am relieved for Officer Banji but what about us? You said many things…how do you know all of this? You can be wrong?"

"Why don't you trust me? He looked at her studied her face and replied. "Yes, you are right, I could be wrong, but I know all of this because

I just called the weather station. They advise everyone to get off the water as soon as possible, for the reason that it may turn to a category 3 or 4 tropical storm or bigger since it is off-season. It could change direction and go towards Road Town and follow to Charlotte Amalie."

"Yes, but Beef Island…"

"Beef Island is not that far away from Road Town Andrea; you know that a storm of this caliber could change to a hurricane and reach a mile wide easily. Just the wind itself around the storm could cause a lot of damages."

They rush the dogs inside the cabin and grab anything that could become airborne and stored it below behind close doors.

"Should we try to put safety vests on the dogs?" Asked Andrea.

"We do not have time to struggle with it, but you and I should definitely ware vest. They sat beside each other at the helm with the dogs at their feet and braced themselves has they raced across the water as fast as they could. Finally, they reached the first bay at Beef Island in less than thirty minutes. Andrea looked at Thomas and suggested since they were so close, they should try to go for it and continue to Long Bay Beach just another few miles. He agreed and they were off again.

As they turned into the last bay, the wind shifted and pick up force as they anchored the boat a few feet from shore. The clouds were getting darker and heavier full of rain and lightning, immediately without loosing any time, Thomas pushed Buster in the water and next Buddy and then jump out after them. Andrea was still on the bow when the boat started to rock back and forth.

"Andrea jump, Andrea jumps now." He screamed at her over the sound of the whistling wind.

"I can't I am afraid."

"Look the dogs are paddling to the shore we must catch up with them before they run away scared." She took gathered her nerves and jump in the water holding her nose. He grabbed her as she came up from under the water and pushed in the direction of the shore.

"What were you waiting for, out there?" He yields at her as they reached the shoreline.

" We are too far from my house; I will never be able to run this fast." Thomas was holding on to his dog in one hand and Andrea's hand in the other as she was trying to hold back Buddy, when Thomas stopped dead in his track:

"Wait, I don't think this is a good idea to attempt to reach your house." He looked around at their situation and decided they should take shelter in the mountain on the west side. As they were trying to climb the mountain the wind picks up and then the rain started, it was coming down so fast it was like a stream rolling down the mountain, the trees, bushes were bending and cracking like twigs, scaring the dogs. Thomas decided the beach would be better and replied has he studding the huge clouds coming in.

"Instead let's go back on the beach behind the sand dunes and try to cover ourselves with anything we can find. Come on, let's go Andrea."

Just below the mountain there was a huge dune and close by was a big tub turned on its side fill with earth and beautiful flowers.

"Come here Andrea, tie the dogs to the tree and come help me with this." He ordered her.

"What, what do you think you are doing?" She asked. And what are you planning to do with the tub."

"We will use it for shelter." He replied without looking at her.

"No, Thomas don't, women who planted these flowers will be furious with you. This is someone's offering to the sea, to return the fishermen safe back home with plenty of fish to feed their family.

"We need it more than the fishermen right now. We are going to empty it and put it over us when the storm starts coming in toward us. This tub (as he was kicking it) behind the dunes should be a good shelter for us. It is heavy enough. Come help me, hurry finishing tying the dogs and help me."

The wind began to howl and pounding waves against the shore. The dogs were crying from the sand getting into their eyes, Andrea and Thomas could barely see or breathed themselves. Andrea found a small wooden box buried in the sand when she was digging in the tub, and she showed it to Thomas.

"Leave it; it probably belongs to a young child."

She pushed it aside and returned to empty the tub. Finally, all the earth was out, and they drag the tub closer to where the dogs were tied and started to position it securely against a tree.

"What about the dogs, will they be hurt by the flying debris?" She asked sadly watching the dog trying to pull free from the rope.

"Well, this is it, the space is restricted and if we want to save also the dogs, we will be very tight, and the animals may react badly and get spooked and run away. So, what do you want to do?" He looked at her and looked at the dogs crying from the sand hitting and pinching their bodies.

She could not take it anymore and went to Buddy who was crying, she kneeled down beside him, gave him a big hug and turn towards Sam as she grab the rope.

"I think we should try and bring them under the tub with us. If we lean the tub closer against two trees sideways it will give us more room, maybe it will work?"

"That is not a bad idea; we may be able to get away with it, if we hurry. Let's try it."

They drag and pull the tub until it was leaning solidly against the trees. They lowered it as much as possible and they all crawled underneath. When they were ready, the storm was almost on top of them. Sheets of rain pellets were pounding against the tub. They each grab their dogs and cuddled under the tub. Buddy being scared of the noise kept trying to run away. Andrea looked at Thomas for help. He reach to grab the dog's collar and missed and hit Andrea on the cheek, he tried again and pulled real hard and the dog started to cry and laid back beside Andrea with his head against her leg to cover his eyes. They tied the ropes to the base of the tree and then tied themselves together.

"Why?" She asks him.

"In case one of us is pulled outside by the force of the wind." He touched her cheek. "Sorry I didn't mean to hit you, are you alright?" He screamed. The noise was so loud that she barely heard him.

"Yes, I am alright." She shouted back with watery eyes.

Thomas was getting impatient being restrained, he decided to untie himself and get up to see where the storm was heading. With the wind blowing hard, Andrea panic and pulled at him to get back down. He stood up just the same, looked around, and came back down as quickly.

"Hold on Andrea, here it comes, it is going to be very serious."

The hurricane started to lash out a load rustling noise and then loader, they held onto the tree, the dogs where howling louder than the wind was making. It became dark very fast; the wind was forcing the tub to move back and fort so much that Thomas was afraid that it might crush them. He grabbed Andrea's hand and squeezed it. "We will be okay, don't worry about it." He winked at her without knowing if she saw it.

They stayed under the tub holding hands for a few minutes but to them it seems like hours, and slowly the wind to die down. They stayed under the tub for a while longer and then tried to push the tub away from them, but something was preventing the tub to move. Thomas slid one foot underneath the tub and hit sand.

"We are sand-in. Help me dig us out."

'How can this happen?"

"The storm just gathered all the sand around the tub when it twirled on the beach and pushed it against it, the same way as for a dune on the beach."

"You mean we have become part of the beach." She panics.

"Push with your feet or take your hands and try to dig an opening, hurry before the dogs starts panicking."

"The dogs! I think I will panic before them!" Her voice was crackling with fear.

They started pushing and pushing with their feet just enough to see a beam of light.

"Close your eyes Andrea" and the dogs finished the rest.

Sand was flying from the dogs trying to get out and soon they were able to push the tub backward and they were free.

Thomas started to look and surveyed the damage, the mountain was totally shaved on one side, debris was all over the beach and for the boat, well, it was gone. Sam scanned the water with his eyes to see if he could spot boat debris but could not find any, there were branches and trees down all around them and the water was a mess. In the corner of his eye, he saw something big bopping in the water about a quarter mile at sea.

"Andrea looks, over there!" he is pointing towards the water. "Your boat is still afloat. It's a good sign."

They ran to the end of the beach to see better the boat and saw it was leaning more on one side, but no other visible damage from where they were standing

"What now? How are we going to get it home if I still have a home?" As she looks on towards the opposite end of the beach where her house was located.

"I will try to board the boat and see if any damages were done to the bottom."

"And if there are damages, what next?"

"Beef Island is a long island; we could always walk towards the other end in the direction of your house and leave the boat there or try to straighten it up and go back to the marina get our cars and go home from there."

"Do you think it's feasible to try and get the boat back up and running?"

"Yes, I think so. We need to try something and level it should not be too hard, according that you have a bilge pump and not too much water in the lower bilge."

"What is a bilge pump?" she questioned. "And it is not my…Ah! Never mind just forget it."

"A bilge pump" He answered. " Is a device, which is used to remove the water from the bilge under the bottom floor! It is where the water from the deck goes, it is a collection point and if it cannot drain quickly enough it is routed into the lower bottom of the yacht under the floor. You start the bilge pump, and it drains it all out through a hole on the side.

"How much water is in there? I really do not know until I get back on it. Come on, let's go see." Thomas removed his shoes, started to undress, taking is T-Shirt off and then is belt and last is jeans came off. He ran in the water towards the boat with the dogs following him. She took her shoes off, started to walk in the water, and stopped. He was halfway to the boat when she decided not to follow him. He reached the boat, went around it to survey the damages, came back to the rear, and saw her standing knee high in the water. He swam back to her.

"So? What are the damages?" She asked him.

"Actually, I can't see any visible damages without going under water to see if it is punctured. What is the matter, Andrea?"

"Nothing" but she could not take her eyes off his nice muscular chest and his lean stomach and tights, she finally rested her eyes on the…bathing suit. He looked at her and smiled.

"What, are you disappointed? Were you expecting something else?"

"Don't be silly." Her face changed to a deep red, and she turned around.

"I just didn't notice the bathing suit when you removed your jeans".

The water was still very choppy and full of debris floating about, she reminded him to be careful. He dove back in. A few minutes later, she started to panic. She looked around to see where he could have surface, but no sigh of him. It was now more than five minutes since he went under water, and she decided she would need to go in after him. The dogs were running in the water looking also for him. She could not take it any longer, she dove in after him and came face to face with him and they both came up coughing for air.

"What do you think you are doing?" He screamed at her.

"I was worried about you; I was just coming to see if you needed my help".

He passed beside her, went around the back of the boat, and started pushing on it to send it sideways.

"What are you doing?"

"Come here and help me! We need to launch the boat in deeper waters".

She swam beside him, placed her hands against the extended swimming platform, and pushed. The boat started to move sideways slowly and eventually straighten up. He grabbed the toe rope and slowly guided the boat towards the shallow end of the west side where a huge rock came out, he signaled her to go back to shore. She swam back slowly as she watched him struggling to climb up the rock. He was just about to straighten up when a huge wave came crushing down on him and he lost his footing and went back under. Andrea screamed out his name, she held her breath and prayed for him to appear, but Thomas was not coming back up and the boat was drifting further in the open waters. She stood there watching the boat floating away with Thomas nowhere to be found.

Standing there all alone with the two dogs, she fell on her knees in the sand, placing her hands in front of her eyes as she started crying. The dogs started licking her face not knowing what was going on. She pushed them away at the sound of motors in the distance, she looked up and saw two, four wheelers coming towards her at full speed, she panics and started to run in the water, calling the dogs to follow her. She swam towards the boat as fast as she could, but the boat was drifting faster than she could swim. She looked back and saw one of the bikers getting off and entering the water. She decided to continue to swim towards the boat, the dogs where getting tired and she could not see Thomas, anywhere. Her arms could no longer do another stroke and she slowly stopped and turn onto her back, she lifted her head to see if the man was still swimming towards her, but he had decided to return to his bike and where now leaving the beach. She decided to return to the beach when she saw her boat slowly coming towards her. She started to scream Thomas's name hoping he was on the boat. She called the dogs to swim towards her. The boat was coming closer and closer but this time she could ear the motor running and saw Thomas at the wheel of the boat. She lifted one arm and waved at him, he slowed down, first, beside the dogs and pick up one and then the other and finally came beside her and gave his hand to her and lifted her out of the water. She got up looked at him and gave him a big hug and then she said.

"You stopped for the dogs before me!"

"Yes, in case I needed protection from you." She looked at him and he continued… "For not telling you I was going back for the boat."

He placed his arms around her neck and kissed her slowly, for a long time. She could barely breed, and he let her go.

"Do you forgive me for now?"

"Hmmmm, yes, yes I do forgive you and I am so glad you are alive. Thank you for coming back for us."

"I am also glad that you made it, but right now you need to let go of me or otherwise we will crash in the rocks."

"Sorry" She blushed then turns her attention towards the dogs.

"Andrea! Come here. Would you like to learn how to maneuver this beautiful toy?"

They both sat in front of the boat and showed her how to steer towards the open sea, gave her specific instruction, explain the control panel the equipment and antennae.

After a few minutes she was, overwhelm. "What does all of that means?"

"It means the controls here are connected to the mechanics below deck with computers. This boat is the state-of-the-art beauty. It could navigate by itself."

As they approach the shoreline, the two men on the wheelers came back on the beach looking screaming insanities at them.

Thomas returned to verify if the bilge was still working, then return to the wheel, and slowly return to St Thomas by following the shoreline.

They saw the bikers also following the shoreline on land, making fist, and screaming.

"After all that commotion, we didn't have a chance to look into the property you own; would you like to come back another day." He suggested.

She replied. "Yes, definitely." She looked back at him with small, tired eyes. "Thomas, have you decided where you will anchor the boat tonight? And what should I do with it, sell it or keep it?"

"We will anchor it at the restaurant, at the same one where police station uses. I should continue the investigation and give a complete inspection to it. I am sure I will not fine anything after all this. Then once it is release, you can do whatever you want with it. He informed her.

"So, I should start looking for a marina with space big enough for my boat." That was the first time she used the word "MY" to describe the yacht.

It was now close to nine o'clock when they arrived at the marina, the dogs where tired and so was the passengers. They loaded all their belonging in their separate cars, and they kissed and kissed and kissed then said their goodbyes without even taking in their surroundings:

"Oh my god! Look at the road, how am I going to get home?"

The top of the road was blocked by a huge tree trunk and at the bottom of the road was washed out. She notices people standing outside on their property trying to free branches on cars and rooftops, a van was turned over in the ditch, rocks and mud was pushed down the road by the water current.

"Now what?" She lifted her eyes and hands toward the sky.

"Ok, let's not panic, we can always go back by boat to your place, correct?" He asked.

"I have no place to anchor the boat remember and the island does not have a marina."

"Actually yes, there is one on the other side at the airport, it is small, it's only for the airport water bus but I could ask if we can park it there and walk to your house, it shouldn't be more than a couple of miles." He looked at her with a smile.

"Just a few miles!" If you did not notice it is dark outside, and, I am very tired!" She went silence for a moment and replied.

"Well ok, anything as long as you can get me home for a good night sleep in my own bed." Once she realized what she had said, she could feel her cheeks turning red and she looked away.

They left their cars in the parking lot of the restaurant, and on their way back to the boat with bags and the dogs, Thomas noticed a young boy running towards them and screaming.

"Senor, Senor necesitamos su ayuda. Pegan a un hombre en su coche y no podemos conseguirlo hacia fuera. Por favor el senor viene.

She looked at Thomas: 'What did he say? 'She asked worried. "His he hurt?"

"No, he needs our help. He said" "A man is stuck in his car and they cannot get him out. Please sir, come." He explains to her with the young boy still pulling at his arm.

Thomas looked at Andrea and shrugged his shoulders. "Lock the dogs inside the boat cabin." He shouted to her at the same time running towards the end of the road with the boy.

"Thomas, wait I am coming with you."

She hurried the dogs inside and started towards Thomas.

He looked at her, smile, she reaches is side, and he grabbed her by the hand and started running. When they arrived at the scene, the man was in his car with all the windows closed. The current kept pushing him further down the hill toward the sea. The young boy was crying, and Thomas figured it was probably his grandfather or his father.

"? Es este su padre?" Asked Thomas to the young boy.

"No, é les mi guarda". He replied at Thomas.

Thomas turned toward Andrea and repeated. "I asked him if it was his father, and he replied not the man is the guardian of these kids."

"Well let's not just stand here let's help."

Thomas tried to free the car door for the older man to get out, but the debris were too heavy, he motioned the man to cover his face and he grab a big log and started banging in the window. Nothing happens, he could not manage to break it.

Andrea shouted. "Try the back window, look there is a small crack, maybe it will break easier."

"Maybe, but how can I get there with all of this debris". Shouted Thomas over the noise and rushing water coming down from the mountain.

Thomas saw that the car was moving slowly down the side of the mountain and if he does not do something soon the man will go over the side.

He looked at the situation again, and instead of the big log, he crabbed a good size rock, took a run for the car, jumps on top of the hood, and crawled over the top onto the back of the car. He started to hit the window and slowly the crack started to get bigger and bigger but not fast enough for Thomas, the car was moving faster now under the current.

Andrea picked up also a big rock and jump where Thomas had jump before and join him.

"What do you think you are doing? Get down from here".

"Two is better than one. Come on Thomas, you know you can use my help."

He knew she was right and bickering with her would be a waste of precious time, time they did not have, they started banging on the window together.

After a few seconds, the window gave away to their efforts and they help the old man out of the car. The three of them were standing on top of the trunk when the car started to move down the hill faster, they jump off and landed in a pool of mud up to their knees.

Everyone was happy, the old man was safe, and the boy was screaming from joy. Everyone joined the old man except for Andrea; she tried to get out of the mud but could not move. She asked Thomas to help her. He leaned towards her and tried to pull her out.

"What is wrong?"

"My shoes are stuck."

"Well try to get out of them"

"What?" Leave my shoes behind!"

"It's you or your shoes make a decision!" and he laughed.

'Funny, just pull."

He finally set her free and barefoot, they all laughed and returned to there respective homes.

Andrea and Thomas returned to the yacht to wash off the mud.

"Are you sure you want to go back on the water tonight? Look at all the debris floating in the water it's getting more dangerous to navigate especially in the dark."

"Yes, I want to go home, I told you I am tired, and I want sleep in my bed."

"Andrea, you have all the necessities in your yacht why don't you just sleep here, if you are afraid I will sleep on board with you."

"No, I want to go home."

They left the marina slowly and manage to arrive at the airport an hour later. He called in ahead to make sure everything was all right for them to dock. Once more, they started to unload the boat.

"Stop let's just leave everything here and we will pick it up tomorrow, I am too tired, what do you think?"

"Yes, it's fine with me." He replied.

It took them exactly thirty minutes to walk to her place; at one point he had to grab her by the hand, she was so tired. At there arrival, the dogs started running and barking at a light shinning at the other end of the driveway.

"Wait here Andrea" Has he pushed her aside behind a tree.

He walked slowly and carefully towards the light and asked the person to identify himself.

"Sir it's me, Officer Banji!"

"Officer Banji! What are you doing here? Where is your car?" He asked and then motioned Andrea to come forward.

"It's ok, Andrea its Officer Banji." He continued.

"Sir, when I saw the hurricane coming towards the islands, I decided to come over and see if Ms. Andrea would need my help, but when I arrived there was no one here, so I decided to stick around and then two men arrived in a white car. I hid in the bushes, and they entered the house by a window." He turned towards Andrea. "You should always lock your windows Ma'am." He turned towards Thomas again and continued is story.

"I did not attempt to arrest them since I was alone and unable to ask for back up. They stayed for about half an hour and left. Once they were gone, I entered the house to check if there were damages made to Ms

Andrea's things, but I couldn't see anything displaced or broken except for this note."

He reached in his shirt pocket and retrieved a piece of paper. He handed it over to detective Pondas.

"Excuse me but I do believe it is my note" As she extended her hand to Pondas, he looked at her and saw she was serious; he paused for a few second and red the note. Andrea was furious she grabbed the note from his hand and red it.

"No matter what you say, you are not staying here alone until this is all over."

"Ok" she replied without arguing after she read the note.

The note said: LEAVE THESE ISLANDS OR ELSE."

"I am so tired of this mess maybe that's what I should do, just leave this place and return to Canada and never come back. All I got since my husband died his trouble over his death and the people he knew. Everyone is being killed or treat because of him. I am just so tired of all of this."

"Don't be silly, everything will be fine, we will arrest these people, and bring them in front of the court and they will be lock up for a long time."

"And then what" she asked and started too walked away."

"Where is your car, Officer?"

"I came by foot Sir; I parked my car at the marina." The officer answered back.

"Ok then, Andrea you can go to bed, Officer Banji and I will stand on watch until morning."

"But Thomas you are as tired as I am. Why don't you lie down on the sofa, and I will bring some blankets and a few pillows?" She left and returned a few minutes later with a sheet, blankets and two soft pillows.

The two men were sitting at the kitchen table discussing the schedule of their watch.

"You will be comfortable on the living room sofa, and you Officer, you can stand watch on the patio. There is a very large hammock in the corner and here is a pillow and a blanket for you. It is turning out to be a beautiful evening so it will not be to damp for you. If so, you can close the shutters on the end."

"Thank you, ma'am, but I don't know if I can rest, if I am standing watch, I will be fine."

Nevertheless, it is very comfortable and thank you… I mean it, thank you for your help, I know you are doing this off duty. It is very nice of you."

She handed over the blanket and pillow, looking directly at him, he returns her a big smile she walked away.

"Good night, Officers" she said without turning around.

Nothing serious happen during the night except around four o'clock in the morning the dogs started barking. She heard Thomas and officer Banji talking and then going outside with the dogs. They all returned about thirty minutes later and the house turned quiet again.

Chapter Seven

The next morning Andrea woke up to the smell of fresh coffee brewing and bacon cooking. She jumped in the shower, washed, and blew her hair, rubbed cream all over her face, arms and legs. She dressed in a pair of white shorts with a tangerine T-Shirt, came down to the kitchen before any one new she was awake. Thomas and Officer Banji were getting ready to sit down at the table when they both saw her entering the kitchen.

"Good morning, ma'am."

"Good morning officer. She replied with a smile.

"Good morning did you sleep well Andrea?" Thomas glancing directly at her legs. She blushed and replied.

"Yes, thank you and yourself, the sofa wasn't too hard on your back?"

"No, it was very comfortable like you said. As a matter of fact, it is better than the one at my office."

"I slept a few hours also on the hammock and it was also comfortable." Added the officer and she smiled at him.

She returned her attention to Thomas.

"Your office, do you sleep their often." She questioned.

"Often enough" he replied by touching is back.

"Did I hear you get up during the night with the dogs, was there someone lurking around the house."

"Sorry did we wake you up? The dogs wanted to stretch their legs and go for a pi. They might have heard a lizard underneath the house or a rat but nothing more."

"A what? Rat…I have rats…aren't they dangerous for my cat and the dogs and they do bit humans? Where is my cat, I have not seen Charlotte for days, even since I got Buddy, I place food out for her on the veranda and it disappears.

"The rat must be eating the food."

Oh! My good, poor Charlotte, her food?"

"Yes, they are dangerous but they will not come around if they smell or see big animals only if there are food lying around the house."

"Then, what were they doing last night, what should I do?"

"Do what?"

She repeated. "What should I do regarding the rats? How can I get rid of them?"

"Don't worry about them. The dog will take care of that. Just letting Buddy out every day, that alone will scare the rats and they will move on to another location if you stop putting food out."

"Are you sure? I am really afraid of rats." She answered and then made a weird face.

Thomas looked at Andrea and smiled. "No there is nothing to be afraid of." He reassured her.

"Officer Banji, did you look around this morning?" Inquired Thomas.

"Yes sir, I went for a walk along the wall area near the end of the island, walked around in the streets of the neighborhood, a saw a lot of houses that have been damaged by the storm, the street is damaged by running water, the waterfront is full of debris, which also explain why rats are coming around. The cleaning up is already started, I saw people racking, cleaned up on the beach."

Did you see Tabby running usually she likes to run after seagulls on the beach?

"As a matter of fact, I did. Could that be your cat? Ms. Andrea"

"Yes, my Charlotte, good she his safe."

"And also Ms. Andrea, the south corner of your house has been damaged by the storm." Added the Officer, and before he could finish is phrase, she should have someone repair it as soon as possible, before the next big rainfall.

"What? My house is damaged." She got up and ran barefoot towards the front door, with Buddy following her and Brutus not far behind. They both raced passed her pushing her against the wall.

"Hey you guys!" She regains her balance and opens the front door. A screech came out of her mouth:" Wowww" when a large man holding a gun in her face surprised her.

The dogs started barking at the intruder. He kicked one of them out of the way. The animal yield and retrieved to the kitchen where Thomas was calling them back.

"Get back in the house bitch before I waste you right here." He screamed at her.

She hesitated and he pushed her. "Get back in…now."

She screamed back at him. "Ok, ok don't hurt me." She tripped on her way to the kitchen.

By that time, Andrea and the intruder made their way into the kitchen. Officer Banji had slowly crawled on the floor and managed to enter the pantry with Buddy on his heels. Immediately Thomas reaches for the dog, grabbed him by the collar before anyone could see what the officer was doing. Banji slowly closed the door behind him, leaving just a small crack to be able to observe everything.

As she walked in Thomas saw the expression of fear on her pale face. Thomas stood up like as if he was surprised to see the visitor, instinctively lifted his arms in the air to show the man he was not carrying any firearms and had no intention of hurting him.

The dogs where fidgety and Thomas ordered them both to sit, but Buddy went directly to the pantry door and the man's gaze followed him.

"What is in there"? He questioned.

Andrea automatically answered. "The bag of dog food is in there. I did not have time to feed them this morning."

Thomas took the lead and responded by: "What do you want?"

The intruder's attention returned to Thomas and Andrea.

"The lady knows exactly what I want, don't you doll?" Said the intruder while he pushed her toward Thomas. She stumbled and landed in his arms.

She straightens faced the man and replied. "I don't know what you want?" Is it the boat, you came for, well you can, have it? It's parked at the airport marina." She snapped at him.

"Shut up, bitch! You know it is not the boat, the house, or the Mercedes. All I want is the deed of the land and the map where the scum of husband of yours buried my treasurer. Tell me where the chest box is and the key to open it and I will be on my way.

Andrea's jaw fell when she heard about the Mercedes and everything else. "Mercedes, deed, map, treasure, what is he talking about?" She looked at Thomas as if he could give her an explanation.

"Stop repeating what I say, you know exactly what I mean, give it to me." He pointed the gun in her face, and she scream in horror.

At that exact moment officer Banji came out of his hiding place and shouted.

"Put your hands up!" the man turned around pointing his gun at Banji and fired, Banji docked sideways and returned fire on the intruder and hit him on the shoulder, Thomas pushed Andrea to the floor. The gunman dropped the gun and Thomas kicked it towards Andrea, she picks it up and handed it over to Thomas.

Andrea started shaking so much that she collapsed on the floor and started crying. The dogs started barking. Thomas handcuffed the man while

Banji called the dogs over and pushed them towards the living room and return to sit on the floor.

Thomas bends over to Andrea. "Are you alright, are you hurt."

"I'm fine; just never saw anyone being shot before."

Thomas left her side to call for an ambulance and a police car.

"What? What do you mean not before two hours? Just send an ambulance right now to." He looked at Andrea for the address and she replied. "1563 St. Marteen Street."

He repeated "1563 St. Marteen Beef Island on the waterfront. He then waited for the person on the other end to repeat the address. "What no ambulance. I have a man with a gun wound and this man could bleed to death." He took a second look at the man and then returned his attention to the person on the phone. "Ok, send an ambulance when ever you have one free. Don't worry about it; we will take care of him."

He returned the phone receiver to its cradle and grabbed Andrea by the arm and broth her closely to his chest. Looking in her eyes he slowly asked her again.

"Are you sure you are alright? You are still shaking." He commented.

"She is a tough old bird; don't worry about her, I heard she killed Nick Santos and his wife." Replied the man while trying to hold his bleeding shoulder with his cuffed hands.

She looked at him. "You're mad. I did not kill anyone."

"Tell us where you hid the key, the chest box, the deed and the map, you know where they are, come on tell us doll."

"You have no evidence that the lady is involved with what her husband was doing or even his business. She is telling the truth. She may be guilty of…" He turned towards her and spoke. "Of being married to the scoundrel." He tenderly squeezed her arms with affection without looking down at her.

Andrea without any response left Thomas's side to get some bandages and solution to clean the intruders wound. She deposited the articles on the counter and looked at Thomas and left again to return a few minutes later with white rags to make a spleen for the man's shoulder.

"Sorry, that's all I have!" She pointed to products on the counter.

She looked at the man and kneeled down beside him, opened his shirt to reveal the wound, the man suddenly moves to adjusted is position and Thomas was all over him.

"Make another move on her and your dead."

She cleaned the blood carefully around the wound with alcohol and was surprised to see only a deep hole. The bullet had exited his shoulder to the back. She started to clean it with care and noticed sitting in the corner was Officer Banji. He was very quiet and pale. She glanced at him and saw him trying to lift himself from the floor and grabbing the kitchen counter.

"Are you alright Officer?" She left the intruder's side and went towards Banji.

Officer Banji sat down again. "I think I got hit?" Mumbled the officer and fell sideways to the floor.

"Thomas, Thomas, come here quick." Yield out, Andrea.

Thomas kneeled beside him and turned the officer sideways, slowly, removed his jacket and saw a large amount of blood under his arm. He had been on his right side. Andrea, instantly grab the solution and the rest of the clean rags and attended to the officers wound immediately.

She turned and looked at Thomas with tears in her eyes.

"It looks really bad Thomas. I do not know if he will be able to wait for the ambulance, please, we should call them back, right away?"

Thomas looked at Banji and then the wound and spoke. "Yes, you are right; he won't be able to wait for an ambulance. He does not look good, he his loosing too much blood. He will never survive if we do not leave for the hospital right now."

"Hey, lady what about me, you're not finish fixing me up yet."

"Shut up, just shut up or I will do to you what you say I am capable of doing. Do you understand me, shut up?" She screamed at him.

Thomas looked at her standing over the man. She was pointing her finger at him like if she was holding a gun to his face.

'Oh! Oh! The lady has a soft spot for the Officer." The intruder mocked her.

Thomas looked at Andrea with an uncertain air and then returned his attention back to the Officer where he was lying down. When he saw Officer Banji so weak and pale, he decided right then, he had no choice but to bring him to the hospital himself. But how? No one had a car at the house, Officer Banji is unconscious, and he left his car at the marina.

"I can't just walk to the hospital with him in my arms, I would never make it." Replied Thomas aloud. "We have no car."

He looked at the intruder for several minutes, and then he started questioning him. "What is your name? Did you come here alone? Did you arrive by car or on foot?"

The intruder answered: "Never mind my name or if I came alone. I know you need me and my car, so let's make a deal here." Requested the man.

Andrea walked over to the man and kicked him in the leg. "Deal, you want a deal. You just shoot an officer, and you want to make a deal"

She kicks him again in the leg but this time with force. "The only deal you will get is you will be brought to the hospital that is it. Now where is your car?" She kicked him repeatedly.

Thomas looked at her without saying a word. He knew she was furious with this man who invaded her space, threaten her with a gun and then shot (her new friend) the officer.

The man looked at her in silence rubbing his leg with a smirk on his face.

Thomas turned toward him and pointed his gun at is leg and said: "I won't kick you, but I will put a bullet in your knee if you do not answer the lady in the count of three.

"One, two." He cocked his gun. "And trrr...."

"Hey, wait a minute, wait stop that. Usted esta loco," Cried the man. "Lady please tell him to stop."

Andrea turned to face Thomas and speaks. "Wait Thomas, I need to block my ears first."

The man screamed again. "Wait, you are both mad. Loco, loco". Has he reached in his pocket and hold his keys to Thomas and told them where he had hidden the vehicle.

"It is a white Chrysler Le Baron older model but with lots of room in the back seat." He replied winking at Andrea.

Thomas grabbed the keys from him and passed them to Andrea.

She looked at the keys, then at him.

"Don't get any ideas Andrea; I will not leave you here alone with this man. You will get the car and while you are gone, I will watch him and let the dogs out for a few minutes and then we will all meet you in front."

The man again explains to Andrea where he had hidden is car. "It is two houses down on the left side of your house, where no one could see it.

"You know the Willows?" She asked.

"No but I know they are gone for a few weeks."

"And how do you know that?" She asked.

"We have been watching your husband for many months now Ms. Karr or Woods what ever name you give yourself now." He replied.

"Watching my husband?"

"Can we please finish this conversation maybe at another time? Andrea hurry, think of Officer Banji."

"I am so sorry; I am leaving at this moment."

She went to the exact location where he said he had hidden the car. It was a big car. She started the vehicle and put it in gear and a after a few minutes she was backing up as close as possible in front of her door. Thomas was already waiting for her outside. The man was handcuffed to the front railing of her steps and Officer Banji was sitting and leaning against the front door.

"Andrea helps me with Officer Banji, we will lay him across the back seat." They managed to place Banji stretched out on the back, Andrea sat beside him with is head on her lap behind the passenger seat. Thomas brought the intruder and sat him in front on the passenger side and handcuff him to the inside door handle. Thomas handed the gun to

Andrea and told her to point it at the intruder's head. He verified all the doors were secure and return to the drivers' side.

Thomas turned to Andrea. "If he makes any kind of move towards me, kill him, don't hesitate for a minute, just do it."

"Shoot him where?" She asked with macabre look in her eye, and he replied.

"Anywhere, as long as he cannot move afterwards, just shoot him." He turns to face the man. "And she will, have no doubts. Like you said she has killed before."

He shifted the car in forward gear, and they were on their way to the city.

Just about two miles before the outskirt of St Thomas the road was a complete wash out. The water was running off so fast from the mountain that it made a canal across the road.

"What are we going to do now; we do not have a moment to spare Thomas?" She looked at Banji lying on her lap and tears started to roll down her cheeks.

Thomas stopped the car and got out without answering her. He started to walk around and survey the canal and it's surrounding. Just a few feet from them, on the other side he saw a small house in the bushes with a scrap yard in the back.

"Wait, I will be back, and, keep the gun pointed to his head and do not hesitate to shoot if he tries anything. You hear me Andrea." She looked at the man and said without turning around. "Don't worry about me."

He looked for a place to cross safely but there was none; he slowly descended in the crevice and walked in the water onto the other side. He walked over and knocked on the door, he waited, and no one was at home. He walked around the back of the house it seems deserted he looked around and found planks of wood and dragged them over to the road where they were all waiting.

"I found these; they will do just fine." He shouted to them.

He positioned the boards across the crevice in the shallowest end and walked over them and jumping at different places to see if it would hold the weight of a car.

Andrea came out of the car. "Are you sure, because we need to go right now, Officer Banji is losing a lot of blood and he looks very pale. Can I help you in any way?"

"No, I can manage, just tend to Banji.

What seemed to be forever to Andrea, Thomas returned a few minutes later.

"We are ready; I think this will hold the car. Andrea, can you guide me across the bridge, just make sure I don't get off the planks."

"What, me guide you, are you sure? He looked at her with a "Come on" look and she replied. "Ok."

She crossed over the makeshift bridge slowly and signaled Thomas to come forward.

"Turn your wheels a little to the left." She screamed.

"Good, now come forward… slowly."

She squatted closer to the ground to have a better of the wheels position: at that moment Thomas panic, he could not see her.

"Andrea where are you?"

"I am ok; I just wanted to see clearly if the four wheels were on the planks."

Inch by inch she guided him closer and closer to the other side. After fifteen minutes of intense worrying if, they would make it or not, the car finally crossed over.

"Ok, you are cleared." She looked at the sky and made a sign of a cross over her chest.

Andrea ran to the car and jump inside. They finally reached the hospital in less than thirty minutes but to them it liked like an eternity. Officer Banji was no longer responding to her voice, and she started to cry.

At the hospital, in the emergency they attendees were rushing back and forth, the emergency room was full of people with cuts, broken limbs. One of the attendees recognized Thomas and rushed over.

"What is wrong Officer?" He asked.

"This is officer Banji; he was shot in the line of duty, protecting Ms. Andrea from that man." He pointed to the man sitting in the car. The attendee pulled a gurney and they laid Banji on it, is face was as pale as the white sheet. A doctor immediately attended to him and instantly rolled him in one of the operating rooms at the end of the hall. Later Thomas returned to the car, removed the cuffs from the man's wrist, and brought him in a private room where he handcuffs him to the bed and asked the security personal to guard him.

Thomas searches around for Andrea and noticed her in the waiting room where he was sitting patiently covered with Officer Banji blood.

"How is he, can we go see him? She asked.

"No not yet, they just rolled him in the operating room. What about you, are you alright" He looked at the amount of blood she had on her T-Shirt.

"I am Ok."

As they were waiting in the emergency, two ambulances came rushing in with four burnt victims. Curious of the injuries, Thomas approached the drivers and questioned them.

"What? You don't know about the flash fire that started after the hurricane." Informed the ambulance drivers.

"What flash fire and where is it?"

"It's North of St. Thomas at St John, a manufacturer of fireworks exploded. And all the hospitals are full of burnt victims, now we are bringing people here with less serious burns." The driver answered.

Thomas returned to the sitting room where Andrea was waiting patiently. Took her hands in his looked her in the eyes:

"Andrea, I need to leave you alone, I should be going back to the police station to see if they need my help with survivors of the flood and now with the fire that just broke out. I will see you soon." He gave her a hug, kissed her on the cheek, and started to walk away.

"Thomas." She ran after him. "Why? Stay with me, please. Aren't you on holidays?" She reminded him.

"Yes, but duty calls, and I need to go."

"What about the intruder, what will I do with him?"

"You will do nothing; I spoke with the authorities and they will be here soon to take over. I will see you in a few days. Take care of Banji."

He winked at her and left in the intruder's car.

She waited for hours sitting alone in the waiting room of the hospital before someone came back and informed her of Officer Banji condition.

"He is out of danger for the moment and resting peacefully, you should go home now and come back tomorrow, and he would be more receptive to visitors." Explain the doctor to Andrea and other man is recovering fine, also in no danger. The bullet made a clean exit of his shoulder there is no infection present due to the good care he received." He explains to Andrea

"That is really too bad!" She replied and walked away.

As soon as she was out of the hospital, she realized she had no means of transportation to return home and did not know where to go. One thing she knew, she had to go back home as soon as possible for the dogs.

She started walking towards the same road they arrived from, looking around for a taxicab, soon after she remembered, her car was parked at marina not to fare away. She started walking towards that direction; two miles later, she reached her destination with a nice sunburn on the top of her nose and her shoulders.

The car was parked beside the restaurant; a few branches where on top of the hood, mud was splattered all over the side and a huge rock was blocking the left back wheel the rest of the car looked fine. She started to push on the rock, but it was pin against the tire, she grab a big branch and started to push the rock sideways and after a few minutes of pushing and pulling she finally got the rock lose and pushed it aside, she clear the top of the car and she was determine that nothing else would stop her now from taking her car back home. She looked around and the road was mostly cleared from debris of the day before. She opened the car door and looked inside for her bag she had left behind that day and changed into a clean T-Shirt.

A few minutes later she was sitting in her car and on her way back home hoping to make it back before dark. Arriving at the spot in the road where Thomas had placed the planks to cross over, she did not know if she could do it, she started to get nervous.

"What if I can't drive in a straight line, what if one wheel fell of the planks, what then? Will I roll over?" She asked herself. She pondered on leaving the car on the side of the road and walk the rest of the way. She got out walked around and looked everything over and decided to continue. She slowly advanced up to the beginning of the two planks and she opened the car door to tried and look if the wheels were aligned but she couldn't see properly. She decided to get out of the car and cross over to the other side. She slowly descended in the rushing water; it was now a few degrees colder, and the evening was approaching fast. She finely made it on the other side, she kneeled and saw her wheels where perfectly lined up with the plank: she returns back to the car. She started to motor put it in forward gear and grab the steering wheel, she slowly presses down the pedal and prayed she makes it across safely. Little by little she advanced, she could feel the weight of the car pressing down onto the board, and then at the point of almost being totally across, she heard a cracking noise. She took a deep breath and press on the gas. She was finally safe on the other side, she looked back in the rear mirror and saw one plank had broken in half, she started crying.

Eventually when she had stopped crying, she got out of the vehicle, picked up the planks one at a time and slowly dropped them in the water and pushed them down the stream. The water came murkier, and they disappeared. She didn't want any unwanted visitors coming to her house during the night.

"Now no one can cross over… Oh! My god what did I just do." She looked for the planks, but they were gone for good.

It was dark when she made it back to her place, unable to move she sat in her car for a while just catching her breath, she could hear the dogs barking and decided it was time to go in, but first she walked around the back of the house and sat on the veranda steps. Looking out at the sea smelling the fresh air she wondered where Thomas was tonight. Feeling sorry for herself she decided to go in and tend to the dogs, she was now worried why they had stop barking.

She opened the back door and went in the kitchen, at her first view on the floor was the amount of blood that Officer Banji and the intruders had lost. The place was a mess and the dogs were lying in the corner beside the refrigerator in a daze.

"Oh my god, what's wrong with you two. The dogs where unable to get up, they appeared to be sleepy and then closer she could smell the rubbing alcohol and found the bottle empty on the floor. She kneeled beside them and smelled their breath, it reeked of the alcohol.

"What, you are both drunk?" She started to laugh.

"What am I going to do with you two?" The dogs were looking at her with half closed eyes and then flopped back down on the kitchen floor.

"You are useless to me tonight: you couldn't defend me if I need it."

"I am too tired to deal with you two or this mess, I am going to bed. I will fix all this tomorrow." And she closed all the lights, coaxed the dogs to go with her but no reaction so she went to bed alone.

When she woke up the next day, the sun was shining, and the air was clear. She blocked the light from her red puffy eyes and rolled over. An hour later she woke up again this time sun was shining on her bare legs, and it felt good and warm. She moved and saw the dogs at the end of her bed, they were both still passed out from the night before.

"She patted their heads, come on wake up, sleepy heads." They slowly opened their eyes and started to lick her face.

"Stop that, she laughs, come on, get up, lost of work to do today."

They all found their way to the kitchen. At the sight of the mess, she immediately opened the back door and allowed the dogs to go out before they started to walk all over the pool of blood. Still holding the door open she looked back at the mess and decided to follow the dogs outside for a while. The morning air was so clean, and they all went for a long walk on the beach and they returned an hour later hungry and thirsty.

It took her most of the day to clean the kitchen to return everything back to normal.

Chapter Eight

A few days have passed since the incident with the intruder and Officer Banji was still in the hospital. She had called every day to obtain information about his condition.

"He is getting much better and stronger every day." The nurse had replied.

For the next few days, she concentrated on returning her house back to normal but with Brutus, Thomas's dog and Buddy running all over it was not easy. She needed to get in touch with Thomas, but how, she had not heard from him since the day at the hospital and she was now very worried.

She kept busy by arranging James boxes in the living room in order by size beside the fireplace. Thomas had promised to look through them with her. "Maybe clues regarding what happen to James are in these boxes." He had commented when he saw them.

After a week, the city crewmen had most of the main roads repaired including her road. She was now able to go back to work at the store. She was grateful to Lana for having kept the store open during her absence and Andrea promised her a few days off with pay after they finish the year end inventory. The next few days she made several trips to the hospital sometimes twice a day to visit Officer Banji. She also decided not to wait for Thomas and started looking inside the boxes in her living room. She was unable to make sense why James would have kept odd knickknack in some boxes. Maybe she could find the mysterious key, box chest any clue about what everyone are looking for.

"But if it's both, a key in a box or in a chest? I must ask Thomas when he comes back for clues to help me solve this mystery."

In the morning before leaving the house, she received a phone call from the hospital. At the sound of the doctor's voice, her heart started beating faster and was afraid of bad news.

"Doctor, is Officer Banji worst?" She asked with a trembling voice.

"No, he is fine."

She was relieved to know that Officer Banji was being released from the hospital the next day. She was so relieving that she offered to make the arrangement to pick him up herself.

That morning, she got up and dressed in a hurry to be at the hospital before he could change his mind and leave on his own. She arrived minutes before eight o'clock in his room. She had brought his clothes home to wash them a few days before and had returned them the next day. He was already dressed in the clean clothes sitting on the bed waiting for his ride.

"Officer Banji, you are up and ready!"

"Ms. Karr!" He replied. "Are you the person who is picking me up?"

"What is this, Ms. Karr, what happen to Andrea and yes I am… disappointed?"

"I am back on my feet and on duty again… yes, I am pleased that it is you picking me up." He mumbled.

"No, you are not ready to go back to work; do you have someone at home… or someone that you know that could take care of you for a few days until you recover fully?" She asked while grabbing the rest of his personal belongings that she had supplied him with during is stay at the hospital.

"No, I live alone in a small one-bedroom apartment close to the station house. Why?"

"Well, then you are coming home with me, and I do not want any arguments from you." She winked at him.

He smiled and followed her to the nurse station where he signed his release.

"Ready?" She asked.

"Ready."

"Not all the roads around the city are quite back to normal but some more than others are more manageable and cleaner of debris." Offered Andrea as she tried to avoid holds and bumps in the road but one, she could not avoid and he let a sound of pain.

"I'm sorry, I'm sorry." She kept repeating.

A few minutes later as they were stopped at a red light, waiting to turn towards center town, Officer Banji replied:

"Andrea, I need to confess something to you!"

"What do you mean, confess?"

"Aren't you a bit curious why I didn't make a fuss about staying with you? Why I agreed without an argument?"

"Yes, I was surprised. But you do need some care."

"Remember when I told you at the hospital that I was back on duty, well, I am. Thomas and I, I mean Detective Pondas and I, agreed that you need protection; we were discussing the arrangement when the intruder came in your house. We decided I should move in with you and Detective Pondas would replace me on weekends. I need to recuperate and can watch over you at the same time. This is the only reason why I did not argue with you."

"He did, did he? What else did you discuss about me"? Her voice sounded nasty.

"Did he what?" He asked and continued. "I would not force you to do anything you would not want but, it would be for your protection, if it's ok with you." He suggested?"

She looked at him in silence and shrugged her shoulders.

"It looks like you are not comfortable with the idea and prefer not to be burden with a sick person, I understand. I will come back once I have recuperated from my injury."

"Don't be silly, of course you can stay with me, I could use the company and I am certain it would make officer Pondas happy."

"If you let me stay, I promise I will not run after or shoot anyone while I am under your care. How is that?"

"Perfect" And they both started laughing.

After making a few stops to the grocery, deli, bakery, and drug store for the pain killers the doctor had prescribed for Banji, she had finally completed her shopping. She had now all the necessary things she would need for her special guest. When they finally arrived at the house it was well after lunch time.

He wanted to help her with the grocery bags but she gave him a {don't you dare} stare.

"Just the small bags, I am sure I can manage those." He replied.

"No." She had insisted.

As soon as she opened the front door, the dogs ran right past her and started jumping all over the officer. Andrea panicked and started yelling at the dogs and rushed them back in the house and ran to open the back door to let them out in the yard.

She returned beside Officer Banji and softly grabbed his arm and guided him to the sofa in the living room.

"Are you alright? They didn't hurt you?"

"I'm OK."

"Here, sit down on the sofa and stretch your legs or even better lay down for a few minutes, I will tend to the dogs and be right back." She helped him to lie down, puffed the cushion behind him and smiled and left him alone.

Once she had walked and fed the dogs, put away all the groceries, she returned to the living room where Officer Banji was still resting to ask him if he was hungry or needed something to drink.

After he didn't reply she came closer to see if he was alright when she noticed he was fast asleep, she picked up the throw blanket from the corner wing chair and covered him slowly without disturbing him. She returned outside, sat on the deck for a few minutes resting her eyes. She was now more worried about what could happen if another intruder would happen to come along and look for what ever they are all looking for, she would need to defend herself plus her guest.

"What did I do, what a responsibility." She whispered to herself.

Few hours later when the sun was slowly setting behind the mountains, she was startled by someone walking in the kitchen. She jumps up and saw Banji walking slowly towards the kitchen table holding his side.

"Hi there, is your side sore, would you like your pain killers now?" She went in the kitchen started to look around for where she might have left them when she unpacked the shopping bags.

"Hi! How long was I out?" He asked.

"Let me see". She looked at her watch. "It has been a couple of hours. Are you hungry?"

"No not really, it is more a thirst than a hunger feeling that I have. Do you have something cold to drink?"

"Yes, I have cold jus, ice water, what do you want?"

"Do you have anything stronger?"

"Are you sure you want something stronger." She had found the pills and was showing them to him. "You are taking pain killers, it is not a good idea, you know it is not recommended to take alcohol with medication."

"Yes, I know. The last time I took a pill was this morning at the hospital and I really feel like a cold cerveza… I mean a cold beer; it would be good now."

"I know what cerveza means." She replied. "And yes, I have cold beer, white wine, Vodka, Rum all in the refrigerator. But I don't know if my beer is your brand."

"Any brand is good enough as long as it is ice cold."

She walked over the refrigerator and grabbed two bottles of beer from the bottom shelf and a block of goat cheese and grapes, she then moved to the cupboards and retrieved two glasses and the box of saltines.

"No glass for me. Thanks, I prefer drinking from the bottle. Do you need any help with all of that?" He asked her has he got up.

"No, sit." She motioned him back to his chair with her hand. "I am ok." She came back to the table deposited the beers, glass, saltines, and cheese and then went back for plates, knifes, napkins and a bowl of assorted nuts that were left on the corner counter the night before.

He looked at her and looked back at the table. "What, no pickles?"

"Pickles?" She repeated had made a yucky face.

"You never had cheese, crackers and pickles with beer before?"

"No, usually nachos with cheese and Jalapenos, but never pickles with beer, my sister did that once, pickles with her beer, and if I remember correctly, she was pregnant, but I, personally never tried it." She replied.

She got up and looked for the jar of pickles in the refrigerator and returned to the table. "It's a weird combination of taste, but if you like it, go for it, they are all yours." And she pushed the jar towards him.

"Only a pregnant woman would eat such a combination." She looked at him and laughed. "Did the anesthesia give you weird taste buds?"

And they both started laughing out loud while Banji hold on to his side.

They sat around the table talking, eating, and drinking until he suddenly asked.

"Andrea, the boxes in the living room, they are from James office, correct?"

"Yes, they are James, but not from his office, they are from his apartment in the city."

"His apartment? You owned an apartment plus a house?"

"No, he had an apartment plus a house; I… had just a home." As she looked around her kitchen.

She paused and then continued after clearing her throat.

"I started to look inside the boxes, but I was waiting for Thomas, I mean Detective Pondas, I just skim over the first one and found only nicnacks."

"Would you like to go through them now?" The office suggested without giving any remarks about her using the Detective first name.

"What do you mean, now…are you up to it?"

"Yes, if we sit on the floor, I think I will be able to manage it for a while."

They finished their beer and moved to the living room. Before sitting down Andrea went back to the refrigerator and grabbed two more beers.

When she returned, she deposited the beers on the coffee table, help him to the floor and rearrange cushions all around him to make sure he was comfortable.

"This is new to me…to be pampered like this; I never had any one to look after me."

"Never?" She asked all surprised. "No girlfriend, your mother must have pampered you when you were a child?"

"No, no girlfriend, no mother, I lost my mother and father when I was three years old. I do not remember them, and I was broth up by the nuns at the St-Theresa Convent in Charlotte Amalie."

"Oh! I am so sorry."

"Why? I am not. The nuns were very nice to me, but, not in a nurturing way like a mother would be."

She looked at him and could imagine this small little boy, losing his parents and place in a cold dark convent with heartless nuns. Andrea did not like the convent life; her father had placed her and her sister in a catholic convent after their mother died. Being a man, he had said that it would be better for them to have feminine influence to go through their teenage years. They were at the convent not more than a year when they decided to run away.

"What is wrong Andrea?" When he saw her expression of discuss on her face.

"It's nothing, just bad memories. Shall we start" She turned impatiently towards the boxes and took the smallest one. They sifted through every paper, pamphlets, red them thoroughly and classified them according to date and place.

They moved to the second box, this book was full of knick-knacks, statuettes glassware, teacups, saucers and utensils, that was the one she had open days before. Some had names of places stamp on the bottom, others had design, and some had small maps printed on the back. They wrote everything down with all the details and set them aside for later.

At the third box and the third beer, they were getting very comfortable with each other and talking about everything from their childhood to now. He asked her personal questions about her and James, how long they were married if they had planned for children; they used the apartment in the city often.

"He never mentioned the apartment, I just found out the other day when his landlady sends him a bill for the rent due for last month and wanted to know if he still needed the apartment and was he planning on coming back.

"Did you know her?"

"I remembered meeting her at one point. She used to own my store.

The officer continued to ask her questions the old woman than the apartment.

"Was the lady a native or an immigrant, was he selling Real-Estate for her?"

"No, she is an old native person in her seventies. She makes blankets and pillows to sell at the peer and I do believe I have also some of her works in my store."

She mentioned that Thomas used to bring blankets and trinkets at the store and said it was from an old lady from the village but he never gave me her name, but he gave her a big wooden chest box in payment for her blankets.

"You said a wooden chest box? And what was it that the intruder wanted? A chest box with a key, was it?"

'I do not think he meant that chest box. This one is huge it's for blankets and stuff."

"Can we go see it?"

"What? Now, it is too late?"

"No not now but maybe tomorrow or the day after."

"Yes, I am sure I can still find the place."

For the rest of the evening, they moved to the sofa, and they were moving more slowly at each box.

At nine thirty Officer Banji started to feel the pain of his injury coming back. He was getting restless, and Andrea noticed the expression of fatigue on his face.

"We should finish the last two boxes maybe another day."

She excused herself and returned a few minutes later with fresh cleaned sheets, blanket, and a soft pillow. She made him a bed on the sofa, she dims the lights to a soft glow and motioned him to lie down on the soft white linen.

He looked at her. "You are a very bossy person you know that!

She laughed. "I am but only when I am sure of myself." She looked at him and gave a motion with her head to lie down."

She walked to the kitchen and came back a few minutes later with a tray combine of a glass of water, his pills and a box of tissue. "Are you comfortable?" Before he could answer, she replied.

"Just a second I will be right back." She ran toward her bedroom and emerged later with a pair of blue pajamas a towel and a face cloth.

"Here you will be more comfortable in these?" She replied with a smile.

"They were James, I hope you don't mind?"

He looked at the fabric and with hesitation took them slowly from her hands and whispered close to her ear.

"I usually don't wear pajamas in bed, but for you I will make an exception." And he winked at her.

She looked at him for a moment slowly repeating in her head what he had just said and blushed.

"Oh! Good night, Officer Banji, the washroom is that way." she quickly walked towards her bedroom door wandering if he had notice her red cheeks.

He softly shouted back at her. "Guardo"

"What? She answered as she turned slowly to look at him, not expecting him to be so close to her.

"My name" He whispered in low husky voice. "Is Edwardo Lutto Banji, but all my close friends' they call me "Guardo."

"Oh! Thank you." And she repeated. "Good night Guardo."

"Good night, Andrea." He took the liberty of reaching for her hand and slowly kissed the top of her fingers. Lifted his head and looked in her eyes.

"May I call you Andrea?"

The only thing that came out of her mouth was. "Yah! Sure."

"Then, good night, Andrea, I will see you in the morning."

At that moment the dogs impatiently pushed her leg as they pass beside her to go to her room, and she lost balance and fell forward. He grabs her by the shoulders and steady her, she was so close to his lips that she could feel the warmed in them. She slowly licked her lips, and he took a deep breath.

"Please Andrea." He begged her, and she closed her eyes and he slowly press his lips against hers, he then placed one hand in the small of her back and press her forward so she could feel how he felt for her. She slowly melted in his arms. With the other hand he caressed her hair gently, he then pulled away and she let a sound of sorrow escape from her mouth. He looked into her eyes and saw she wanted more. He bent over and kissed her neck and slowly worked his way to the front of her open blouse. Her body was rubbing against his and he… let go.

"What? What is wrong, you do not find me desirable?" She asked all perplexed.

"Andrea!"

"Oh! I am sorry, did I hurt you?" and she touched his side where the bandage was showing.

He pushed her away.

"No, I am not in pain, well not the physical pain! Andrea, I am working for you, I am supposed to protect you, this would not be appropriate. You could interpret it as I am taking advantage of you."

"What nonsense, pure nonsense, I would never think of such a thing!"

She turned and followed the dogs to her bedroom and closed the door behind her.

She changed to her nightgown and went to use her ensuite bathroom from her bedroom when she heard Guardo washing up; he had entered by the hallway. She returns to her bed and pick up her book on the side table and started reading, but her mind kept going back to Guardo, she drop the book on the bed and return to the bathroom door, she softly knocked.

"Guardo are you alright." She waited for him to respond, she could hear him swearing and moaning of pain. She wanted to go to him and help him, but he had not responded to her call. She decided to give him a few minutes more while she would go back to her book. She returned a few minutes later, knocked on the door one more time, she presses her ear close to the door to listen for sounds. There was none, she decided to slowly open the door.

"Guardo… Are you alright…do you need my help?" He was sitting on the side of the tub, leaning against the wall, with beads of perspiration coming down his forehead.

"Guardo…"

"Yes, please…I do need your help." He was barely able to stand.

She wiped the beads of perspiration with a cold face cloth.

She left him for a moment and returned with a small vanity chair, she placed it beside the tub and helped him to it. Standing in front of him she knew he could not return to the sofa for the night. His fewer was back and he needed attention. She slowly washed his face with cold water, wipe down the front and the back of his neck. She talked Guardo into letting her remove his bandages and examine his operation. He grabbed her hand and she looked at him. "What is wrong, am I hurting you, I am sorry, am I not doing this right?"

She immediately slides one leg between his two legs to be more solid on her feet and gently lifted his arm and placed it over his head. She bent forward leaning toward his side to check his back and wiped with cold water. Her breast was rubbing against his chest every time she would move. He could feel her contracted nipple against him, and he pushed her away.

"No, you are not hurting me, and I don't think this is a good idea for you to continue. I may be sick and feverish, but I am still a man. Looking at you in that sexy nightgown is not very good for my blood pressure right now."

She kissed him on the forehead, and he grabbed her by the waist and pulled himself up. "Please, you are killing me." And he gave her a peck on the cheek. "Leave I will do it myself."

"Don't be silly, sit down and just look away or close your eyes while I dress up your wound and I will be finish in no time."

She finished dressing his wound and washed his face again and helped him up.

"Thank you." He kissed her on the forehead. Slowly turned and was heading for the sofa when she grabs his hand and pulled him towards her room. "No, this way."

He looked at her with an air of (no, not tonight, I have a headache) king of look.

"Don't flatter yourself officer." She replied when she noticed the expression on his face. "I just think you would be more comfortable in a soft bed instead of the sofa."

He leaned over and softly kissed the corner of her lips. "Thank you."

She pushed the bedroom door open and walked over to the bed with him, pulled the covers and extracted a few decorative pillows that she knew he would not need.

She looked at him. "Is this, ok?" She waited until he was settling down and closed the light behind her and returned to the bathroom.

She tidied up and slowly took her time to wash her face and brushed her teeth. She returned to the bedroom, softly touched his forehead and noticed he was asleep. She pulled the covers up to his neck and pushed the dogs of the bed. She then went to sleep on the sofa.

In the early morning, she quietly dressed and went to the bathroom to wash up; she slowly opened the bedroom door to check up on him, but only to find the bed empty. She hurried to go through James's closet to find clothes for the officer. She found a pair of blue jeans and a pale blue Golf Shirt from the boxes she had stacked in the back of the closet. She had left them there for a reminder James, but she knew one day she would bring them to the charity box at church.

She unfolded the jeans and shirt to examine them more carefully and automatically she brought the clothes close to her face and smelled them. They smelled of James cologne, she pushed them away from her face. The image of him being unfaithful to their marriage vows left her angry towards him and she resented that.

She regains her composer and looks at other pieces of clothing and found stockings and underwear. The underwear she discarded but, the rest she neatly placed them on the bed. She decided to also change into a pair of slimming jeans and a sleeveless top and continued her grooming, brushed her hair in a ponytail, applied cream on her face and hands and lipstick on her swollen lips from the night before. She quickly walked towards the kitchen where the smell of fresh brewed coffee filled the air.

"Good morning, how do you feel this morning? Are you sore? I have laid a change of clean clothes for you on the bed, you are welcome to them. I am certain they will fit. You are about the same size as James (she cleared her throat) …was."

"No, and thank you, I am much better, the pills are really doing their job, and for the clothes, I will look at them later." He replied and handed her a cup of fresh java. Their hands touched and they both stop…they looked at each other for a while and he was the first to say.

"Sorry. Today… I shall run over to my place and pick up a few things if I am going to stay here with you for a while. I will need more clothing and my razor." He said has he touched his face gently.

"What did you do at the hospital for a shave?"

A nice nurse shaved me since I couldn't lift my arms" He looked at her.

"Are you offering to do the same?"

She turned to hide her blushed cheeks. "Maybe" She replied and changed the subject: "Are you up to travel by car for a long period of time, today?"

"Yes, I should be ok…I checked my bandages this morning and every thing looked dry. Thank you for taking such good care of me, you are a very caring person should have been a nurse." He continued. "With a few pills I should survive the day just fine."

"If your bandages are dry that is a good sign, right? Did the doctor mentioned when you will need to go back at the hospital for your check up?"

"Yes, he said in six days that should bring us to the beginning of next week, and at the same time he will remove my stitches and pass an X-ray for my lungs."

"That is good news. Excuse me, I will be right back."

And she left him in the kitchen to call Lana who should be at the store by now. She informed her that she will be away for a few days and if she did not mind being alone at the store. She would appreciate it.

The young girl was pleased that Andrea trusted her to do so. Andrea promised her when she returns and everything is back to normal, she would allow the young girl to take a long holiday and will be well compensated for all the good work she was doing for her at the store. She also mentioned if any suspicious person or package arrives at the store to call her immediately at home or on her cellular phone.

She returned to the kitchen and advised him he had her full attention for a couple of days. After breakfast Guardo excused himself and went to Andrea's room to change into what she had left for him on the bed. During that time, Andrea kept herself busy by making several folders of all the papers they gathered the night before and sorted them by date and stores. She also made a list of places to visit and why James would have bought different diving gears and other articles.

When he returned to the kitchen, she saw this beautiful tan body in tight blue jeans; he was still holding his shirt in his hands when he walking in the kitchen. She could not stop staring at his tan body; the pants fit him perfectly, even too perfect. They were hugging his hips and tights, she could see a bulge in front that she never noticed with James when he wears the pants... She pass her fingers in her hair slowly and kept on staring, he had to move sideways to break her stare. She looked up at him and blushed of embarrassment. She walked up to him and handed over the list she had made for him. He looked at it.

"He never mentions the yacht or the diving gear or maps to you, he never brought you diving during your marriage?" He continued questioning her has he handed the golf shirt over to her.

She looked at the shirt and then at him.

"What, not your color?" She replied sarcastically.

He laughed. "No, it is not that, I can't pass it over my head. I cannot lift my arms to high, can you help me?"

"Oh sorry." she felt uncomfortable. "Would you like a shirt with buttons instead?"

"No, this is ok; I just need help with it."

She took the golf shirt and slowly guided his hands in the arm holes and then struggle to pass it over his head. He had to squat down lower for her to direct it over his head. She had to stand facing him closely with her breast touching his face.

They both stood still for a minute, and she adjusted his golf shirt and he slowly stood up, he adjusted his pants.

Then she broke of with:

"Once we went diving at Great Camanoe Island before we were married, it was on our second date, we were with two other couples, I am pretty sure one of the couples was the Santos and the other couple, I had never met them before or never saw them again. We pass the day on the boat; the guys dove for several hours. I believe it was Nick Santos boat and then we all went for a meal at the Anegada Hotel. That is all I remember of that day"

"You said there was also another couple? Do you remember their names?

"No, I don't remember their names but, the lady was older than the gentleman and, you may think this is silly, but the gentlemen resembled Detective Pondas, but younger and he had a red baseball cap and a moustache."

She was silent for a moment and then shouted. "A baseball caps!"

He looked at her with a puzzled expression. "What about a baseball cap."

"Now I remember why red baseball cap keeps popping up all over town around me. Maybe this guy is the one who killed James and the Santos."

"Are you sure that you do not remember what the woman or the man looked like?"

"Definitely the woman I never saw again, because I would remember seeing her, she was a tall, dark, very beautiful, a Spanish native."

"You said you were not married when you went diving, that would bring you before 2005?

"I guess around that time. Why?"

"I am not sure yet but, I may have a lead on the case."

"Oh! Detective Pondas will be happy, he keeps saying that he wants to bring this killer being bars and finally put to rest this case and I also will be happy to know that James's killer is finally punished."

"Andrea, please don't say a word to the Detective before I have all my proofs, I would not like to give him wrong information, you do understand, don't you?"

"Yes, I do no problem." And she smiled back at him.

They left right after cleaning up the kitchen and walking the dogs.

First on their list was Mrs. Medina, James's landlady.

"Guardo?"

He was surprised how his name came so easily to her and it felt good hearing a woman say his name again.

"Yes, Andrea." He replied and she continued.

"Can we stop at my store first before we visit Mrs. Medina; I need to get the books to complete Lana's paycheck and the order supply folder for the month purchase and shipping."

"No problem."

They packed everything they needed and a few minutes later were on their way out the door.

"Should I drive, or will you?"

"If you are up to it, sure you can drive! Thank you." And she handed him her car keys.

Officer Banji negotiated the street of the city with ease, but Andrea noticed he was also speeding at times and slowing down at other times. He was also looking in the back view mirror a lot.

"Is everything alright Guardo?"

"I am not sure yet!" It looks like someone maybe following us."

"What! Not again! Why can they leave me alone?" As she started to turn to look out the back window, he immediately stopped her by putting his hand on the side of her face like a caress.

"Don't look back. He ordered her. "Sorry if I touched you, but I wanted it to look natural in case someone is following us."

"It's ok. She mumbled all shy.

She kept her face turned toward him as if they were in deep conversation but, they were both silent. She looked at him with examining eyes and for the first time she noticed that Officer Banji was rather a beautiful man. He had shiny black hair and nice clean olive skin color with big deep black eyes. The light bleu Shirt against his muscular skin made him look more attractive although you could see fatigue and pain around is beautiful eyes.

Slowly she returned her gaze to the road, thinking if he could only hold her hand it would make it so much more real.

"I will park the car behind your store is that alright with you? If someone is following us, we will be able to see them pass by." He explained.

They arrived in the parking lot and position the car in a certain way to see traffic or people on foot go by without being seen by them. They lowered the seats in front and waited. After a few minutes of comfortably talking about their plans for the day, they heard a car approaching. They crunched lower, waited, and then slowly Officer Banji lifted himself to the window to see more clearly. At that precise moment a white car rolled in closer to the back door, he laid is arm across Andrea's chest to pin her down and then removed it to place a finger to her lips as she was just about to say something.

"Shhhht, they are in the parking lot!"

Andrea looked at him with big eyes filled with fear and tears; she reached for his arm and squeezed it hard. He had to pry her fingers of his arms, to reposition himself in his seat, he looked at her and she had her eyes closed and was praying, which she didn't believe him since a very young age. Andrea was not a church going person but, God, she may believe in or a Mighty Being who existed to protect good people from evil.

Officer Banji lifted himself once more to see what was going on and saw the car moving slowly towards them and stopped at the sound of the back door opening. One of the men got out and lit a cigarette and started talking with the other man in the car. He could not hear what they were saying but it looked like the man standing outside decided to check the back door of the store. He played with the handle for a few seconds and saw it was locked. He waited a few minutes and decided to return to the car. Standing beside the car he waited for a few minutes. Officer Banji slowly lifted one of his pant legs and pulled a gun from his boot. Andrea shifted her weight and made a noise. The man turned around looking directly at Andrea's car and started slowly walking toward it. Lana at that moment opened the back door of the store and shouted. "Hola!" The two men screamed back at her "Buenos dias la Senorita, como van? Veranos el proprietario de este establicimiento?!

She giggled and replied that she was not the owner of the store, but the store clerk and the owner will be coming back soon if they need to talk to her to come back later and she closed the door and locked it. The other man motions his buddy to come back to the car, they talked while finishing their cigarettes then tossing their buts on the ground and left.

While Andrea collected herself Guardo calmly got out of the car, looked around and motion her to follow him.

"What are you going to do now? What are they looking for?"

"If I knew I would tell you but only James would know what they are looking for and since he is no longer with us, they figure you have all the answers." Andrea looked at him with tears in her eyes and ran to the back door. She reached in her purse for her store keys and opened the door, and, immediately closed it behind her without looking if Officer Banji was following her.

Once inside she hurried to her desk and gathered all the material, she needed to do her work from home. She then moved to the front of the store and saw Lana occupied with customers. She waved at her to get her attention and mimic with her mouth "Hello and Goodbye" lifted her books to show Lana why she was there and blew her a kiss and has she return to the back door; Lana came running after her.

"Ms Karr, Ms Karr."

"What is it, Lana?"

"Two men came around the back to see you. They did not leave their names and I told them you would be here later. Is that, ok?"

"Yes, Lana it's ok, but if they return tell them I have left for a few days to go to Anegada, this will keep them away for a while."

Lana looked at her and smile. "Are you going away on holidays Ms. Karr?"

"No. I just do not want to talk to the men at the present time, ok?

Thank you, Lana, please lock the door being me. Bye." And she left to join officer Banji; he was bending over and picking up butts of cigarettes.

"What are you doing, what are those dirty things?"

"These dirty things as you put it will help me identify the men by their DNA. Not me personally but, the lab will, it should make it easier to arrest them after. For the first time we have evidence that you are being followed and we can identify them. So, this, my dear, will answer all of your and our questions about the murder of James Woods, Mr. and Mrs. Nick Santos and maybe more. This should hurry up the procedures and to close the case before anyone else gets killed.

"Why is everyone so interested in this treasure? All of we know it may not exist."

"Well, I hope for your sake its real…in more than one way."

Curious of is remark she couldn't help but to ask. "What does that mean, in more than one way?"

"First, you will get rid of those banditos after you, and second, you will inherit the treasure, if it really belongs to your late husband."

"What do you mean IF it belongs to my late husband? Do you think he may have found a rare treasure that already belongs to someone else, or he may have stolen it from someone?"

"Honestly I do not know what is anymore, and I can't wait to solve this mystery and lock up all of these people behind bars."

He placed the cigarettes buts in a torn envelop that he took from the trash can and placed it in is jean back pocket. He verified the back door to make certain if was properly locked and were on their way to Mrs. Medina.

"This way is faster."

She grabbed his hand and shoved him towards the broken wooden fence.

"Where are you taking me?"

"If we leave the car in the parking lot, the men will think we are still in the store." Cross over and then continued. "The last time I visited Mrs. Medina, I went through here and it was just across on the other street."

"Clever."

"I noticed the broken fence about two months before James died. I had mentioned it to him and said, ("Just leave it, one day I will get to it.) He never did."

"Could it be James broke the fence deliberately to get to his apartment faster?"

"I am not certain but, remembering the way he answered me when I bugged him to fix it, now I would not be surprised."

As they arrived in front of the house, Andrea asked if he also wanted to visit James's apartment.

"We will see if it is necessary. Is that Ok with you, it does not disturb you to know he had another life apart from yours?"

"Sometimes it does and other times I just feel angry that he didn't trust me enough to confine in me."

They arrived at the back door, knock twice and the old lady opened the door with a stick and waving it at them.

"Wow, hold it, I am a policeman, put your stick down. Lady put your stick down or I will do it for you."

He showed his shield to the old lady, and she somewhat calm down.

Mrs. Medina, do you remember me, Andrea, James's wife."

"James?"

"James Woods, the man who rented your loft over your garage!"

"Jamie! Yes, I remember Jamie. Where is Jamie?" How is he? I haven't seen him in a long time."

"Mrs. Medina, Jamie is dead, remember, I came over to empty is apartment last week."

"Jamie is dead?" The old lady seems lost in her taught and suddenly came back to us.

"Hi! What can I do for you?"

"Hi Mrs. Medina, can I see your wooden chest that Jamie gave you?"

"A chest, who are you? Oh! I know who you are, Jamie's wife."

Andrea and Officer Banji both looked at each other in confusion.

"Yes, Mrs. Medina, the wooden chest."

"Do you remember if you have a key to open the chest?" Asked the Officer.

"Why does everyone think I need a key to open the chest?"

"What do you mean everyone? Mrs. Medina.

"Earlier two men were here looking for the key. I didn't like them, they looked like hoodlums. So, I told them that there was no key. The chest was given to me open."

"You do not have a key?" Asked Andrea.

They old lady looked at Andrea and winked. "I never said there was no key.

I was surprised you did not ask me about it before when you came over to gather all his belongings."

"You remember me?"

"Yes, I do, you looked so mad at Jamie at day."

"Mrs. Medina, Jamie is dead, and I don't know why, all I want is to solve this mystery around his death."

"Sit down, I will tell you what happen." The lady pointed to a bench on the porch. They looked at each other had obeyed the old woman.

"About three months ago this young man came running into my backyard and he was followed by two big men. I motioned him to come in and he rushed inside and waited until the men were in the back yard and silently left by the front door. That was the first time I saw Jamie. A few days later, he came by again and this time alone to thank me for saving him from the tugs. He started to explain that he had found something of value and was not clear in is mind what to do with it. He wanted to return it to the proper owner, but who was the proper owner? We talked for hours and then he asked me if I could rent the loft over my garage for a few months to hide it until he could decide what to do. The loft was empty and for rent so I gave him a key and the next day he moved in with a few boxes and suitcases.

Andrea was sitting there with big eyes listening to this woman talking about her husband and telling her all these things that she didn't know about him.

"He would come over two or three times a week, but never slept over." She continued. "And one day he arrived with a big wooden chest and gave it to me and said if ever a beautiful woman comes over and asks for a key show her this chest.

Andrea and Guardo glanced past the old lady and looked at the chest in one of the kitchen corners.

Guardo ventured and asked: "Do you know why he told you that, and did he tell you the name of this beautiful woman?"

"At that time, I didn't know what he was talking about, but the day you came over and told me you were Jamie's wife."

Andrea cut her off. "James, not Jamie. James was his name."

"What ever" The old lady answered and continued her story.

"Then I understood what he meant by showing you the chest. You remember the reaction you had when I told you Jamie gave it to me."

"No."

"Well, I may be old, but I remember, you were amazed by the craftsmanship of the wood design and I asked you if you wanted it back and you said no. And you asked me if I kept it locked with and old key. I told you no it holds only blankets. Well, you see the key Jamie gave me does not work for that chest. Has you can see now, the keyhole is recent and the key he gave me is old and rusted."

"May I see the key, please, Mrs. Medina." Asked the Officer.

"Sure, but you still won't know for what it is good for."

"And you know, for what the key is good for, Mrs. Medina?"

"Yes, young man I know what it is good for and I am not sure if I should tell you."

The old lady went inside for a few minutes and emerged with a small wooden chest box that looked like an old 18th century royal box and with a rusted key.

"This is the chest that Jamie was talking about. Inside the big wooden chest was this small chest with the key tape to it."

"Did you open it?" He asked her with a grin.

"I am old not dumb, young man. Yes, I opened it; inside there was only a torn map of Beef Island with a red square in the middle."

"May I see it?" Andrea asked.

The old lady gave Andrea the small box and the key. She tried to force the key in the opening of the box, but it didn't fit.

The old lady looked at her in amazement. "I didn't say the key opened the small box, dear."

"I don't understand then, what does this key open?"

"That my dear I don't know, but the small box is not locked, it's just sticky to open."

Officer Banji reached for the small box and slowly pried it open, inside was the map like the old lady said and a small bottle of sand.

The map was Beef Island and a big square showed parts of land with lines dividing into properties. One of the parts had a small square on it.

"Let me see. This looked like the property of the deed that was given to me by Mr. Santos or should I say by the late Santos, remember on the beach."

He looked at her and said softly. "I was not there that day; it was Detective Thomas Pondas."

She looked at him and saw something in his face, was it sorry or envy, whatever it was she was not ready to deal with.

Chapter Nine

Andrea slowly got up and left their side to walk in the beautiful garden behind her house. Looking at the beautiful flowers made her completely forgotten these last few days and she was wandering about Thomas. Where was he, what was he doing, is he alright, is he hurt? It was more than a week since she saw him at the hospital, no calls or messages, where can he be.

Guardo left her alone thinking she needed quite moment to think about James. He later joined her, standing by her side slowly touched her shoulder and she jumped.

"Sorry I did not want to startle you, but the old lady asked us to leave now. She said she is tired and had a very active day and needs her rest."

"Oh! Yes, she is right we must go. I should thank her for all her help." She turned to speak with the old women, but she was already gone in the house and was closing the door behind her.

"It's ok; I told her we appreciated all her help. Look." He handed her the small chest.

"Where is the key?" She panicked.

"It's inside the box, what is wrong with you, why is this key so important? What do you know Andrea? Is there something you are not telling me…I mean us, the authority?"

"No, don't be silly, it's just that all these weeks we have been looking for clues and now we have the key and one step closer to the puzzle. I don't want to lose it.

"Now we have the key, but we do not know what it opens, we are no closer than we were yesterday."

"How can you say such a thing? We have a map and a key."

"He looked at her." So what? That does not tell us why your husband James was murder and who killed him?

"Oh! That reminds me." As he was going through is pants pocket looking for something. He pulled the cigarette butts and waves them at her. "These will help us in determining who is following you and maybe we will have answers about your husband's killer."

They started walking towards the store parking lot when at the end of the street was a white car speeding down towards them. He pushed Andrea inside the broken fence, and he followed her.

"Hurry gets in the car." He ran past her and started the car before she even had a chance to open the door. He had the car in gear before she could close the door. They were speeding down the street and turning corners like they were in a Hollywood movie.

After a few minutes of going in and out of side streets and alleys they finally arrived at the police station.

"Come on." He told her.

"Where?"

"What do you mean, where, here inside at the station?"

"Why?"

"Andrea, don't be difficult, come on."

"I need to have this process as soon as possible before any cross contamination." He was holding the envelop with the cigarette buts inside.

Andrea did not like police station, ever since she was brought in for questioning about Nick Santos' body found on the beach with the deed of a property on his chest. At first, she was a suspect in the killings. She didn't trust anyone now, for the exception of Guardo and Thomas.

"Andrea, please come on."

"OK, ok, but I am not staying long, I hate this place. Guardo, why can I stay in the car and wait for you here?"

"He looked at her and pointed to the end of the road where a white car was parked."

She looked past his fingers and frozen at what he was pointing and jumped out of the car and rushed pass him into the police station.

They were inside no more than an hour. Guardo made a report and filled the evidence and the chef inspector called Guardo in his office for more details and they both immerged a few minutes later with a serious look on both of their faces.

"Mr. Woods. Chef Inspector Nochaze" He handed his hand out to her. "I am replacing Detective Thomas Pondas on this case. We will take care of you, don't worry."

She hesitated and gave her hand to the inspector. "What do you mean you are replacing Detective Pondas, is he ill?"

"No, no nothing like that. He had to leave the country for a while on a big case in North America."

"Oh! My case wasn't big enough for him, is that it?" she sarcastically replied.

"No ma'am that is not it, he made sure that everyone cooperated with you and especially office Banji and also to give you all the manpower you are needed to protect you and solve this case."

"Did he, how big of him" She turned around and started to leave.

"Andrea wait, Inspector Nochaze is not finish talking to you."

"What, I think I have heard enough, and I want to leave now, let's go."

"The two officers looked at each other and the Inspector replied to Guardo.

"Ella es una mano por complete!"

"Si y mas." Officer Banji offered.

She turned and looked at them with smoking eyes. "I understood every word that you said, I haven't been in this country long, but I did learn the language and no I am not a hand full and you Guardo what do you mean by… and more?"

The two men stood there with their mouth open and surprised.

"Now what is it you wanted to tell me Inspector?"

"Well first I am sorry for our remarks it was not meant to be insulting. Mr. Woods you will not be able to return to your house for a while, well at least until this case is resolved."

"What?" she turned to look at Guardo. "What does he mean not able to return to my house for a while. What is a while… a few hours, few days, few weeks, months? What?"

"You see". He continued. "I cannot afford to lose officer Banji or yourself for that matter, and Office Banji is still recuperating form a bullet wound injury and needs care. This…could endanger his life and yours. So, I am placing you in a safe home for the time being."

"A what? Safe home…compared to what…?"

"Andrea don't be difficult; we are thinking of you".

"She looked at him, and she could tell that the event of the day took a lot out of him. His skin was pale, and his eyes were in pain and for the first time he was holding his side. She turned her gaze to the inspector and replied. "OK, I will do it, but I am doing this only for him. He has put his life in danger for me and now he is in pain because of it."

"What, Ok. Just like that. I don't believe it. You are not going to try something are you?" Guardo replied.

"No, I am not going to try running away if that is what you mean. I know when I am losing a battle, and this battle I want to win, so I need help from all of you and if being sent to a safe house will help, then I will go. But…"

The two officers looked at each other waiting for the rest of her response.

"My dog, what about the dogs? What will happen to them?"

"What about the dogs, what dogs?" The inspector shouted at Banji.

"Ms. Karr has a dog and babysitting another dog belonging to Detective Pondas."

"What is going on here? How come everyone is involved and I was not told anything". Shouted the inspector.

"Sir, it's a long story and I promise I will write everything to the smallest detail in my report."

"OK, now bring two officers with you and go to number three."

"Number three; is it safe enough for Andrea and her dogs?"

"No dogs… I believe Detective Pondas and his father owns a farm near by. Return Detective Pondas dog to the farm and bring Ms. Karr's dog also. Ask him to keep the dogs for a few weeks.

The inspector seemed to replay a scenario in his head and replied. "Office Banji, you may be right about number three it is not quite safe enough, move her to number five." And he left.

"Number three, number five, what does it all mean?" She asked.

"These are places for people under the protection program. They are houses secluded and well guarded by officers in civilian clothing."

"And I will be going to this number five for a long time?" She questioned.

"It depends on how fast we catch these people."

"I will need some clothes and personal belongings."

"Don't worry everything is taking care of."

"What?"

"As we speak, someone is going over to your place and packing everything that you will need and more, they will bring the dogs with food and their special toys to the farm.

"I am expected to stay there for several weeks. I will miss my dog and my home."

"I will bring him over to visit you sometime." He offered. "And number five will be our new home."

She looked at him and blushed.

"Yes, I will be living with you. We will be portrayed as man and wife. If it's ok with you, that is? Usually, the scenario would be brother and sister, but you can deduct why that is not possible." And he looked at his arms and returned her a smile.

"Are you sure" and she started to laugh. It was something she had not done in a long time. Laughing out loud and she felt good.

"So…when are we going to this home away from home?"

"Right now, if it's ok with you?"

"I have no choice, do I?"

She grabbed his hand and he looked at her and pulled away...

"What are you doing?

"If we are going to be man and wife, I think we should start right now to practice so it won't feel awkward later on. Don't you agree?" And she squeezed his hand.

"OK, I understand, you are getting back at me for what I said back there with the inspector. But you must agree you are a handful at times. I am not used to looking after young woman with a mob of people trying to kill her."

"What? You never had a murder on this island before?"

"No not recently, I think the last murder was back in the 80's and I was not an officer yet. This is a very peaceful Island. Ships full of tourist come and go daily. This keeps our economy growing. We do want everyone happy and returning to our island. Surviving each day and maintaining a good quality of life, we need to get along with each other and all this for food, shelter, and schools for our kids.

"Look I am sorry if I have disturbed your peaceful community and I am trouble to you and your superiors, but my husband was killed and I just want to know why and go on with my life, here or somewhere else. I do not care about any treasure he may have found, you or your community can keep it."

He looked at her and handed her a white scarf. "Put this on."

"What? You are not serious!!

"Yes, I am.

"Ok, but can I at least wait until we are in the car."

"This is the car". It was a small European car, she looked at him and then the car and took the scarf from his hands and place it over her eyes and tight it behind her head.

They travel through the city and then slowly he turned the small car in the driveway of a big house.

"This is number five, wow!!!"

"No, and you are not supposed to peek." and he continued towards the rear of a large garage and slowly maneuvered the car between two huge pine trees and beyond was another dirt road. They stayed on that dirt road for more than thirty minutes.

"Can I take the blind fold off now? I don't know why I had to be blind folded. I'm not the bad guy, you know?

"Yes, ok you can remove it now. And you know it is for the other people protection. All the ones that are forced to live here for years. We do not want to expose these people to outsiders unless it is necessary and since your stay will be only for a few days or weeks, well you can understand why all the precautions.

She removed the fold and was pleasantly surprised of her findings. "It's nice." A small village with a dozen of houses built in the early 90's. On one corner a small theatre, across the corner a small chapel with a cemetery in the back, further down the road, and hotel, a restaurant, grocery store and a drugstore.

He parked the car in the driveway of a beautiful stone house with a large swimming pool in the back and a garden.

"Andrea…Later I will need to leave you alone, and I don't know when I will be back."

"But you are supposed to be with me, remember! You are my husband." She replied with a lump in her throat.

"Yes, I know I am supposed to be your pretend husband, but, I also need to work, remember I am investigating your case, and it's not easy to come and go here." He explained to her.

I promise I will keep in touch with you, I will return soon but you need to understand all my come and goes are necessary.

"Yes, I understand, I think!

After dinner, they decided on a walk around the neighborhood, this would help her get familiarize with her surroundings and expose them to others as a couple. Afterwards he left around seven o'clock on that Tuesday evening to go to the police station.

She waved goodbye and blew him a kiss wondering if she would ever see him again, he waved good by and blew him a kiss. "Well, isn't it what a wife does to her husband when he doesn't know the next time, he will see him?" He said to herself.

For the rest of the evening, she felt restless and went for a swim in the huge swimming pool in the backyard and then went to bed. For the most part of the night, she tosses and turn with vision of her and…sometimes with Guardo, other times with Thomas swimming and enjoying each others company.

The next morning, she got dress and went for a walk, usually at this time of day she would be walking her dog on the beach, today, she was walking alone. She met a few of her neighbors and chatted for a while. Before he left, Officer Banji reminded her of several topics she was allowed to talk with her neighbors: the weather, the flowers in various garden, the stores in the neighborhood and if she likes the house she is staying and any other that is all. He had said, "Small talk, nothing personal."

The next few days were uneventful except for one late afternoon around supper time, she had decided to past the evening outside starting with relaxing in the hot tub. She brought a glass of red wine, a plate of crackers and cheese and a book she had found the library. The tub was placed at the far end of the yard near the north fence, it was quite and very peaceful, the trees were in bloom and the smell of honeysuckle and roses filled the air. She was sitting in the water slowly sliding up to her next in the warm water and she closed her eyes. It felt good to be alone and relaxing. Sipping slowly on her wine she heard a soft low sound; it was more like a young child sniffling. She sat up and lean against the side of the tub to be able to hear more clearly, she was stretching her neck to be closer to the fence when the neighbors Jim came outside and shouted.

"Laura come in the house, Laura, please don't make a scene. You know that one day it would come to this. Laura, stop crying and come in the house."

"No, leave me alone." Screamed the young woman. You are a liar; you told me that you loved me."

Andrea sat there without moving a muscle and she could not believe her ears, a real live drama enrolling just beside her place.

"You said you would stay with me after everything was settled and I was free to go home. I remember that is what you said it."

"Please Laura" the man begged.

"I am free now; I can go home. You said you loved me, and you would bring me home."

Andrea could not believe what she was earring. When she met the young couple yesterday, they looked very happy, and now the young lady is leaving, meaning Jim must be an officer. She tried to listen but also at the same time not listening at the same time, but the curiosity was taking over, and she finally gave in and leaning a little bit more dangerously closer. She heard the officer move, he was now beside Laura, they were sitting on a garden swing, and she could hear her trying to console her and slowly he persuade her to move inside the house. For the rest of the evening Andrea was going through her own scenario and wondering if Detective Pondas would still be around once the murders are caught or would she be with Office Banji whom the likes very much.

The following Saturday she was sitting quietly on the sofa in the living room watching television when she heard a car door. It didn't disturb her because she knew the guy next door had rented a small moving van and add left earlier to go to the store, he had stopped by to asked her if she needed something at the corner store. She returned her attention to the movie she was watching when the doorbell rang, and she jumped. She got up and went to the window and softly push the curtain, she saw a car was parked in front of the house, it was not one she recognized, and she then looked through the peephole and couldn't see anyone. She started to panic, she looked again and still no one was at the door. Suddenly she heard someone playing with the back door. She crawled on the floor and made her way to the kitchen door and lifted herself slowly to look through the curtain and no one was them.

"What! Am I going crazy, did the doorbell really rang and did the handle of the back door made any noise"? She asked herself was she so afraid that her mind was play games with her, still sitting on the floor when the front doorbell rang again. She rushed over to the door and scream out load.

"What do you want? Who is it?"

"Andrea opens the door?"

He stood there holding the doorknob, frozen. Can it be him?

"Who is it?" He asked.

"Andrea, hurry open the damn door…please."

She opened the door and saw a man standing there with a long beard and long hair.

She automatically reached for the door frame and started to close the door when the man stops it with is foot. He kicks it open, and she screamed.

"Stop it." He said and grabbed her by the arm, she pushed him and kicks him as hard as he could, but he was stronger, and he pulled her close to his chest and with one hand raised her face to him and kissed her hard.

She couldn't breathe and for some reason she didn't want that stranger to stop, she was in a man's harm and loving the passionate kiss he was forcing on her. But who was he?"

He pushed her away and closed the door behind them.

"Who are you and what do you want, and how come you know my name?'

"What do you always kiss stranger with such force. You don't know who I am, and you are returning my kiss ready for passion! What kind of woman have you become since I left you?"

"What?"

"It's me Thomas."

"Thomas?" "Is it really you?"

She stood there in front of him looking straight in his eyes, but she couldn't remember what he looked like all she could see were his dark eyes looking back at her.

"Are you alone?" he asked has he looked around.

"Yes, I am alone." "Why?"

"Never mind why?" and he swore underneath his beard.

She couldn't believe how he changed, and his voice was so harsh and he sounded so mad. Was this the real Thomas J. Pondas? He looked tired and his clothes were all dirty.

"Can I come in? Can I go and take a shower and change."

She looked at him and she could tell he was tired and would do him good to go for a shower. "Yes, upstairs the bathroom is fully equipped with shower and towels." She pointed toward the stairs at the left.

I know my way around, thank you. She went back to sit in the living rooms continued watching TV.

She could ear the shower running and then him walking around in the bathroom. An hour later this beautiful shaved and somewhat shorter hair man came down the stairs in a clean pair of jeans and a T-Shirt.

He looked at her. "Oh! I hope your friend won't mind me taking a pair of his jeans and a T-Shirt, their a bit tight fitting but they will do."

"No, its ok I am sure he won't mind." She replied without giving him any other details about her guest.

"What happen to you and why were you gone so long without giving me any news of your whereabouts." She reprimanded.

"I told you I needed to go help the people most hit by the hurricane. You…It looks like you were busy?"

"Don't change the subject Thomas. I heard you were in America not in the Islands helping people." She barked at him.

"Who told you that lie, Guardo? He mocked.

"Actually no, it was Inspector Nochaze at your precinct. And to answer your question, yes, I was very busy but not the way you are implying. I was almost killed again and Guardo helped me a lot and now he is looking for James's killer."

"Guardo, hmm! I may have been away too long?"

"I mean Officer Banji." She quickly answered.

"I know who Guardo is; you do not need to explain to me." He answered back.

Are you hungry?" She asked as she moved towards the kitchen.

"Yes, I could use some food. What do you have?"

"The only thing I have in the frig is leftover pizza and leftover Chinese food."

"Hmmm yummy?" He replied sarcastically.

"Look I wasn't expecting any one tonight. Do you want some or not?"

"Yes, I guest its better than nothing."

She couldn't believe what she was earring, the way he was talking to her. Was he liking that way when he left or has, he become this angry man in a couple of weeks?

They sat at the kitchen table for hours talking and explaining what had happen in the last few weeks. Around one o'clock in the morning Andrea decided that it was late enough, and she was going to bed.

"Where are you staying, are you going back to where you were or going back home or staying at the hotel down the street?"

"What? No, I am staying here with you, I had orders to move here and be your chaperon."

"You are what? No, you are not staying here. I am supposed be a happy married woman."

"Yes, I heard. But Guardo can not come back right away, and they believe you need protection."

"What happen to Guardo is he ok?"

"Yes, Guardo is ok, and I will be his lost brother returning from missionary work and helping victims from hurricane disaster around the world.

'The chief inspector told me you were in America on a special case.

"Oh! That is also true, I just came to see how the case was progressing and I am returning tomorrow back to America."

"What do you mean, why then you said you were here helping people hit by the hurricane, I don't understand, which is it, you cannot be at two places at the same time?"

"Andrea we will talk tomorrow. Go to bed and I will stay in the small room at the end of the corridor."

"What!" As she turned around. "How do you know about the small room?"

"Andrea I was here before on several occasions, like I said before. You are not the first woman alone to stay here."

"Oh!" She looked at him for several minutes and then retreated to her bedroom. Once in bed she felt so lonely and wishing for Guardo to return.

What she had once felt for Thomas before he left, it was no longer there. It was completely different now; Thomas as changed, and she did not like what he as become.

The next day, she prepared breakfast for them and went for a swim and a long walk alone. Most of the time spent together, they didn't talk about anything serious especially between each other. It was more about the case and the dogs.

Later that night she received a phone call from Officer Banji.

"Hello Andrea! Can you meet me tomorrow night at the local hotel; I need to have a talk with you privately without Pondas knowing about it?"

"Hi, you know about." He cut her off. "Don't mention my name Andrea; please just do has I ask. Meet me at eight o'clock tomorrow night. I have critical information on his where about for the past two weeks.

"OK…bye."

The corner hotel was a beautiful place with a relaxing lounge she had gone there once and enjoyed it. The lady next door had brought her for a drink after their walk one evening.

"Who was that?" He asked curiously.

Without hesitating she responded with a lie. "It was the lady across the street, three doors down, she wants to go for a walk with me tomorrow night."

"You know not to say anything about your case or to get too familiar with the neighbors! Do you? And at what time are you going for this walk?"

"God it is just a walk! She replied furiously. "And it's around eight o'clock, OK?"

"Late?"

"Well maybe she knows that every night after supper I go for a swim."

"Again, not good. Do not create a routine…Didn't they mention anything to you when they drop you off?"

She looked at him and escaped to her room to decide what to wear for her walk (meeting) with Guardo and then she retired early with a book.

Chapter Ten

For the next several days, she needed to be on her toes and keep ahead of Pondas questions. In the morning Pondas decided to go for a walk explore and the sites. They visited the chapel, restaurants and the local pharmacy. Andrea found this very strange since he had mention to her he had stayed in the same house before, but without any arguments she went along with him. He bought several small meaningless articles at different places. Things that were not needed things they had already in the house.

When they returned at the house he replied. "Now you have something to talk about tonight with the lady. These are objects that are not personal and without any connection to you.

"What? Talk about a toothbrush, a pack of gum. Oh! And I should not forget the blue pen that you bought for me today. Are you insane? I am a well-educated woman I know how to keep a conversation without talking about myself or my family." She looked at him and whispered to herself. "Asshold" and walked away.

"What did you say?" He screamed out at her.

And she screamed back at him. "You heard me."

She passed the afternoon in the backyard occupying herself with the garden and going for a swim every time she would anticipate him starting a conversation with her. Later that evening, she prepared dinner and went for another swim just before getting ready for her eight o'clock walk with her neighbor and left without saying goodbye to him.

When she closed the door, she knew he would be watching her from the living room front window and spy on her. Once in front of the house, walking up the walkway to the front door, she noticed the yard gate was open and she went by the back. In the back yard she looked around to see if anyone was out there and close the gate behind her. At the other end she saw an opening in the corner, she walked towards it and escape through the fence, when she reached the other side, she noticed it was the street where she was having a meeting. The hotel was situated at the corner of her street with the front door facing her house. She stood their trying to figure how to enter the hotel without being seen by Thomas. Suddenly a big delivery truck stops at the corner light blocking the view of her house, she rushed towards the door and pushed herself in without looking back. Inside the hotel she looked around and saw no one except a man sitting at the other end in a dark corner, she looked again and to her surprise it was Officer Banji already sitting and waiting for her with a glass of red wine.

"Hi" she said with a big smile. "What is this?" She was pointing to the glass.

"What this! It is a husband meeting his wife for a night out and ordering her favorite wine, is it not what a married couple do together when they love each other."

She blushed.

"Did you already forget about us being happily married Andrea?"

She looked at him and smiled.

"Thank you for the red wine…why the big mystery and in the darkest corner of the hotel lounge?"

"I have something to tell you, it is very important that you keep it to yourself. Remember the Chief Officer said that Detective Pondas was going on a big case out of the country?"

"Yes, he said he was going to America but yesterday Pondas told me he was helping the hurricane people on the island."

"Well, he was gone but not to America or helping the hurricane people, but actually, he took your boat out to sea, where and why no one knows. He came back late a few nights ago. The owner of the restaurant was cleaning up for the next day when he saw Officer Pondas parking your boat. He went to the dock and started talking with him. Pondas mention that the both of you were preparing to go on a long trip and that he offered you to take care of having your boat overhaul before leaving. The owner of Hibiscus restaurant found it very strange when Pondas asked him not to mention it to me or to the Chief Officer, that he would be advising them himself. The owner called the Chief Officer and he called me to ask why I was not at the safe house with you and was everything ok."

"Why would he say I was leaving with him for a long trip in my boat? You do not believe him, I hope?"

"Well, he is with you at the present time; nothing is stopping you to leave with him."

"Honestly Guardo" she took a sip of wine and looked away.

"Andrea come closer and give me a kiss". He whispered.

'Please do has I say." He whispered again. "Do not turn around, someone is watching us."

"She bends over and kissed him on the corner of his mouth, and he grabbed her arm gently and pulled her closer to him and held the kiss for a few seconds and has she was pulling away he pulled her back again for a full open mouth kiss.

He let her go gently and replied. "No, I do not believe you were planning on leaving with him."

She dropped back into her seat and smiled at him.

"What am I going to do now?" She asked him with a soft sexy voice.

"Go back home and just do your normal days without getting too involved with him and I will try to get you out of there as soon as possible."

He got up and extended his hand and helped her to her feet, they walk hand in hand towards the front door. It was getting darker now and the streetlights where not on yet.

"Which way did you come from?"

"I am supposed to be taking a walk with the lady from the third house across the street from us."

"Ok, returned and go back home. I will walk you over as far as I can without being noticed."

He kissed her again on the lips and she returned it with passion and finished it with a big hug.

"Hurry back I am scared, he is not the same man as before."

She returned home and Thomas was sitting in the wing chair facing the window pretending to watch TV.

"Did you have a nice walk? He asked sarcastically.

She wondered did he see her with Guardo coming out of the hotel or was he just fishing for information to make her feel insecure.

"Actually, we didn't go for a walk, we stayed in the back yard, she has a big garden swing and we had a glass of wine and we talk, girl talk. Good night."

She ran up the stairs afraid that he would challenge her to discuss what they talked about. The next day they didn't speak a lot but when they did it was cold and short.

"I guess the romance is over." He replied.

"What! What romance?" See replies acidly. "I didn't know we had one."

He looked at her for a long time and she returned his look. "I will be leaving you tonight and I don't think I will be returning. Office Banji is capable to oversee your case from this point on."

"Oh! You're leaving again, and you won't be back?"

"Yes, I just said to you I am not coming back. I am being relocated in Cuba for a couple of months and from there I don't know where I will be going after."

"What about your dog Brutus?

"Well, you can do what ever you want, keep him or leave him with my fathers, I don't care."

"That seams easy for you to just discard of him, is it the same way regarding women you go out with, you just discarding them."

"We were never a real couple and I know you have feelings for Banji, so what is your problem, you are not alone. Don't give me this abandon girl look. I know you and Banji met tonight, I have friends around here."

"Is this why we went around store to store today, so they would know what I look like and be able to spy on me. Ok, yes, I do have feelings for Guardo, he stayed with me and we looked after each other when you disappeared.

He got up walked towards her, stop about a foot in front of her stared into her eyes for a few seconds, bends over and grabs the bag on the floor and walked out the front door.

She stood there for a few minutes wondering what had just happen and where was he going? Was he going to steel is boat again?

She wanted to call Guardo, but she didn't know how to reach him, so she decided to follow Thomas. She waited until he crosses the road and got into a black sporty car. He drove away and she ran outside and jump in her car. She followed him out the village without knowing if she would be able to remember how to return.

She saw him slowing down as he turned to maneuver between the two pine trees. She closed her headlights and waited. He slowed down and flags the other driver to stop. They talked for several minutes and then he drove away, the other car came straight at her. She immediately opened her lights for the car to see her; he just missed her and continued. A few minutes later she saw headlights in her rear-view mirror approaching fast behind her. The car reached her and started to give her the high beam for her to stop, but she was afraid of whom it might be, and she didn't want to loose Thomas. After a while she couldn't keep up with Thomas and the car behind her was not stopping with his lights. She slowed down on the side of the road and also the other car. The man came out of his car and was coming closer to her; she automatically locked her car and rolled up her window. She was just about to step on the gas when she heard a man's voice screaming her name. She looked behind her and saw Guardo walking towards her. She rolled down her window and was just about to say hello when he immediately started on her.

"What do you think your doing? Don't you know it's dangerous to drive without lights and you are not supposed to leave the village?"

"I was just following Thomas. I think he may be involved in James's case; I need to know how."

"Andrea, please let us do our job, don't do this and go back to the house before it is too late!"

"What do you mean before it is too late and what where you are talking about with Thomas just now?"

"If you must know he said that he had a date with a girl in the city and it was over between you too and he is not coming back."

"But…that is not true." She replied.

"Andrea, I am sorry he told me to tell you about the other woman."

"That is not what he said to me. Well about being over with me, yes that is true but another girl…more like another partner."

"You know he does not love you anymore!"

"It's more like, I don't love him anymore?" She looked at him and smile.

"Come on, Guardo get in the car, we need to follow him."

"We…no you are going back to the house."

"If you do not get in the car he will escape, and I will never know the truth about James. Please Guardo come with me and get in, or I will go alone."

"Ok but I am driving.

They finally reach the street: "Ok, which way now, North or South?" He looked at her waiting for an answer.

"North"

"Why?" he asked her, and she quickly responded. "Because may house is that way and I would try to look for the key one last time. They turn the corner and at the next light there he was, waiting for the light to change. As soon as the light changes, he turned going toward the Hibiscus restaurant.

"Oh no, I believe he his going for your boat."

"Why would he do that?" She asked.

"I have two ideas, and you will not like what I am about to tell you… We are probably ninety percent sure that James and Pondas were together in a jewelry heist and were about to do the selling transaction when someone got greedy. Detective Pondas and James, your husband, were going to meet with the buyer when something went wrong and the buyer panic and came after them. James your husband was preparing to take you away in your boat and relocate on another island.

"So that is what he wanted to tell me and Thomas well probably that is why he got close to me, he wanted to know if James gave me the key. He knew if I was in love with him, I would trust him with my life."

"When he realized you didn't know anything about James double life he then decided to go on his own. He was with James two months ago; your husband went to him for protection from the sea pirates."

"Sea pirates! Come on, they don't exist anymore, and why did James went see Mr. Puccino to investigate a matter or was it for protection."

"Did you read the report of Puccino?

"No, not yet why? Do you think the answer is in that report?"

"Did Thomas read it?" He asked.

"I don't know but we need to see where he is going."

They both decided to follow him at a safe distance. When he stopped at the restaurant and went in, Officer Banji knew what he was up to.

"There is a back door to the restaurant just beside the men washroom that comes out onto the marina dock. He probably saw us following him and he is going to run for it."

They parked the car at the end of the parking lot; he picks up is cellular and called for reinforcement.

"What are you doing Guardo? You do not know if he is guilty or innocent and if he has is side arm with him?"

"I know, and don't worry, I won't hurt him. All I want is some answers. Don't you?"

"What! You think I care about him? Well, you are wrong, it is not true, there is nothing between us anymore."

He looked at her and he softly caressed her arm. "I am glad." He then returned his gaze to the boat.

Few minutes later they saw Thomas climb up on the boat. He started the engine and Officer Banji looked around if he could see the patrol cars coming. He could no longer wait for the reinforcement and decide to go after him.

"Guardo, please don't". She pulled on the side of his shirt, and he pushed her hand, looked at her.

"Don't worry I will be back for you. You understand why I need to do this? We will never be free if he gets away. You will always be afraid of him coming back for you."

He quickly opens the door and started running towards the boat.

Slowly, she saw the boat backing up from the deck and Guardo still running down the ramp and to her surprise he jumped on the bow of the boat. She screamed when she saw him slide sideways going in the water and he caught the railing and pulled himself back on the boat.

The boat pulled away and she got out of the car as the patrol cars arrived, there were two cars with four policemen.

It took her five minutes to explain to them what was going on and they radio into the coast guard.

They waited patiently on the dock and later after two hours of looking at the sea, they finally saw lights on the water coming towards them.

Slowly they could make out two boats and one of them was the coast guard and the other vessel was a private boat. Finally, she saw it, her boat. She was relieved to see Guardo at the control.

The policemen met the boat and one silhouette descended, but which one of the two, was it Thomas or Guardo. When Thomas passed beside her, she could see he was handcuff. She looked at him, but he did not look at her. She started to walk slowly towards the boat and only policemen and coast guard police were passing her by and then she saw him Guardo came out talking with an Officer who was patting him on the shoulder. Good job Officer Banji, good job. Guardo thanked the Coast Guards and wave goodbye.

He slowly took his time to walk towards Andrea, when he reached her side, he bent over and kissed her hard on the lips and she slowly responded and then she gave herself to him with joy. The kiss lasted several minutes and when they separated, he informed her, he had to go to the station house to processing Thomas.

"This should take a few hours, it is now close to midnight, and you should go home, you are tired and cold."

She insisted on going to the station with him and was ready to wait for him if it took.

"I do not want to go home alone again, I will wait for you, we will leave together I am not finish taking care of you."

He looked at her and offered his hand to her.

Few hours later they were on their way back home.

Chapter Eleven

On their return Andrea noticed that they were not exactly returning to her home but returning to the safe house.

"Guardo what are you doing, you told me we could go back to my place?"

"Andrea please, one more night will not make a big difference, here or at your home." Explain Guardo. "And tomorrow we will gather all of your belongings and be on our way home early; we will even pick up Buddy from the farm."

"And Brutus" she added.

"And also, Brutus if you wish?"

"Guardo when you say we and home…do you really mean it."

"Yes, I do." He grabbed her hand and brought it to his lips and kissed it gently.

During that evening even though they were both very tired and emotional, they decided to go for a swim. They relaxed and cuddle in the water and then they transferred to the hot tub, he slowly untied her bikini top and as he was kissing her breast she whispered in his ear.

"Let's wait until we are in our bed to make love for the first time."

He looked at her with small sexy eyes and she insisted one more time and he agreed, and they both returned inside the house and went to bed in separate bedroom.

After a few minutes into the night, she heard him scream.

"You know you are killing me slowly."

She laughs and replies. "Just one more night and it will give your injury time to get better, because I promise you will need it."

The next morning, they both got up at six o'clock all packed and ready to leave. When they came down the stairs, they looked at each other. "Ready?" they both said at the same time.

On their way back they stop to pick up the dogs, it was not easy for Andrea to see Pop and not say a thing about the events of the night before. When they arrived at the house it was just before lunch time. A police car was already there waiting for them.

"Officer, what is the problem?" Guardo asked the young man.

"Chief Inspector wants to see you both at the Station House A.S.A.P."

"Can we unpack first and have lunch and then we will go?"

"I am sure the Inspector will not be pleased to know that." He replied.

"What is so important that it can not wait a few hours or one more day? I was there late last night until early hours this morning."

"I am sorry Sir, but I have my orders not to come back to the Station House without you two."

"Ok, we will follow you."

"Guardo what about the dogs"

"We could take them with us. What he as to say should not take to long and we could go for bite to eat afterwards."

"It's fine with me; I see no problems with that."

They all jump back in the car and headed for the Station House.

An hour later they were sitting in the Inspector's office listening to what he had to say.

"You are not serious, he escapes. How did he manage that?"

"Easy he pretended he just booked the murderer of James Wood and asked the officer coming in from his sift work to open the cell door. Sometimes he would go in a cell and sleep there."

"What? Andrea could not believe what he was saying. "Why would he sleep in a cell in a prison, he said he was sleeping in his office?"

"Actually, he started that just before your husband died. He told everyone his apartment was being sprayed for bugs."

"Do you think he was preparing his eventual escape at that point?"

"I think so, he probably knew that soon or later he would be arrested, and this would not look suspicious."

"You can not be serious Guardo! That he would make believe is house is being sprayed to sleep here and give him an excuse to prepare is escape. Now what?

"Now, we should be very careful until he is back behind bars." He replied has he took her hands in his.

"Thank you, officer, I am sure Ms. Karr will be very careful and please let her know of all new charges arising from this event.

"Why are you talking to him like you are going away somewhere?' Asked Andrea with a shaking voice.

"Because I am, I will not rest until I find him and this will mean you will be on your own for a while." Explained Guardo.

"No! You will do no such thing." Voiced the Inspector in Charge.

"I am sorry Sir, but I need to do this, I will not be able to rest until we find and charge him."

"No! Repeated the Inspector. "As of today, you are no longer on this case and you are going on vacation for two weeks. This is an order Officer Banji."

He looked at the Inspector without saying a word knowing it was futile to even ask why and he knew the inspector meant to take Andrea with him. He took Andrea's hand and they left.

Back in the car, Andrea asked Guardo why he did not argue with the Inspector, and that she was mad at him because of it.

"This case needs a lot of leg work and being on vacation will just give me more time to do the research." He explained.

"Guardo, I want to be with you and help you with this."

"Andrea this could be very dangerous, I do not know how many people are associated with this strange case, how many more people will die before we know exactly what is at the bottom of this story."

"I don't care I want to help you, and this also mean I can pass more time to know you better." She smiled at him.

They stop at a roadside restaurant with a small terrace where they where allowed to tie the dogs to a tree and give them food and water. While keeping an eye on the dogs, they planned their next few days and were happy to be together and relax with a glass of wine.

Arriving late at the house, they notice the front door was slightly open.

Guardo immediately let the dogs go, he knew they would rush for the door and as predicted they open the door with their noses and entered.

Guardo immediately stopped Andrea from stepping out of the car and asked her to stay until he cleared the inside.

Nobody was inside, although it seemed that someone had come in and robbed her. The house was a mess, and all of the evidence boxes were missing. When Guardo returned outside to informed her, she was nowhere to be found. He heard a car speeding at the end of the road and started to run after it. His heart started racing at the though of her being kidnapped. He ran back to the car, as he was turning the key Andrea turned the corner of the house asking him where he was going. He looked at her for a moment and jumped out and ran towards her. He grabbed her by the waist and lifts her high enough for their lips to touch. He kissed her repeatedly with passion so much so that she was afraid that he would make love to her right their on the hood of the car in the driveway.

She pushed him. "What is wrong? Are you alright?"

"I am now, when I came back out and saw you were no longer in the car, I assume you had been kidnapped by tugs."

"What? Are you crazy? Why would you think such a thing? Don't worry about me!"

"But I do, I love you and I want to take care of you." He admitted to her.

"You do!

"Yes, I do."

She smiled at him and returned his kiss with more passion that she ever imagined she could show in a kiss. They walked back inside hand in hand, talking and laughing when she stops abruptly at the site of chaos in the living room.

"What happen here?" She started to cry. "Why?"

"Well darling, now they will leave you alone."

She looked at him. "What?"

"Well, whoever did this he or they took all the evidence away with them. All off James boxes from his apartment are gone."

"Good" she said snubbing and whipping her eyes dry. "Like you said they will leave me or us alone now.

They pass the best part of the rest of the afternoon and night fixing the place. While sitting on the sofa, looking around to see if there was any trace left of the entire or deal, she noticed she forgot to dust the small cabinet in the corner. She got up and picked up the dust rag and went over to the cabinet, while dusting it she remembered that James had bought it for her as a wedding gift. He had said it was a French Key Chest from France.

"Guardo" She screamed. "Come quick, please come quick."

"What Andrea, what is the matter."

"Look" She was pointing to the cabinet. "Do you know what this is?"

He looked at her like if she had lost her mind. "Yes dear, it is a cabinet."

"Yes, but not just an ordinary cabinet, its French Key Chest cabinet."

"OK, that is nice."

"No, you do not understand Guardo, a French Key Chest." She repeated.

"What did the note say, a key in a chest or box?"

"Key Chest" He repeated.

"Yes." And she started to open all the drawers and examine the inside. The first one had papers and several pens and pencils and writing paper.

Second one had tablecloths and napkins and the third one had some of James newspaper clipping from diving expedition around the world.

"Did you find something relating to where about is the key."

"No. I was sure the cabinet had something to do with it."

"Do you want me to take it apart?" He offered.

"What do you mean by taking it apart?"

"Well let us start by taking the drawers out one by one." He suggested.

The first drawer was smaller than the other two and it came out easy. They emptied the content on the floor and looked at every side.

The second one was a little large than the first one, again emptied the content on the floor and examined it from all sides. The third one was a little harder to remove but again nothing. She kneeled in front of the cabinet and entered her head inside the empty shell and looked all around the inside and the outside panels. On the left top corner of one of the outside panels there was a large piece of grey tape stuck to the top. She pulled on it and a key were stuck to it with a small piece of paper.

She looked at him and smiled.

"Could this be it?"

He looked at her and lifted his shoulders as if he was saying: "I don't know what it says?"

"It says this key will open your future."

"What does that mean, it will open my future?"

"It is just an ornament key for this cabinet, the drawers do not have a keyhole only the top part of the chest and it does not open. We tried when James brought it home."

"Try again." He suggested.

She placed the key in the keyhole and tried to turn it to the right, nothing happened and then she turned it to the left and she heard a faint click.

"Did you hear that?"

"What?"

"The click, it made a clicking sound, did you hear it?'

"No, I did not. Try again."

She turned it to the left and nothing happen. "I know I heard something."

"Ok, well what did you do before turning the key?" He asked her.

"I turned it to the right and then to the left."

"Well try that again."

She replaced the key in the keyhole and turned it slowly to the right and then slowly to the left and they both heard the faint click and something drop to the floor.

They both bend down to look underneath the cabinet and, could not believe what they were seeing. It was the biggest diamond that anyone ever saw; it was as big as an egg, it was in a note.

"Oh my God!"

"You can say that again!" He picks it up with the note and handed it over to her.

"I do not want it. You keep it."

"Well at least read the note." He said to her laughing.

The note said as she read it out load:

Darlings enjoy yourself. At this point you must know about the yacht the Mercedes, stock and bonds with a large some of money in the safe at the New York Condo on First Avenue. Thomas Pondas will help you find the owner of the diamond for a small fee, trust him.

"Trust him, trust Pondas, he knew James, they were together on this."
She was furious. Guardo had a hard time to calm her down.

"Andrea, you know that we cannot keep the diamond. The rest is yours. This is the reason why everyone is looking for they key; your husband must have found the diamond in one of his diving expeditions with Pondas and was trying to sell it on black market. He must have been holding it until they could find a good buyer for it.

"A what, a buyer? Why?"

"You just can not go to a jeweler and ask if they want to buy a diamond of this size in exchange for money. This is probably worth a couple millions of dollars."

She fell on the floor when she heard the amount.

"Millions, then there is no mystery why he was killed. It was for this diamond."

They finish putting back the cabinet together and tried to relax the rest of the evening. They did not know what to do with it, so, they hid it in the dog food bag. That night they both stayed awake unable to sleep and jumping at every cracking sound they heard.

When the morning came, they rushed to the Station and handed over the diamond to the Inspector.

"What is this?" He could not believe his eyes on the size of the diamond.

She explained that James did receive a lot of money and bought real estate, cars, stocks, and bonds. They passed the entire day at the station she answered all their questions, especially how she found the diamond and where, if she told anyone else about it. Guardo explained he was with her at the time of the found and by her expression he can vouch that she did not know anything about it. The Inspector did not care about what Andrea received has result of money James Woods would have received, all he wanted was the diamond to be returned to the real owner and have his Island return to normal and no more killings. Although the investigation was still ongoing, they let go Andrea that night with Officer Banji.

They returned to her home and were able to relax as much as they could when the phone rang. Andrea got up to answer.

"Hello, what! Who is this? What do you want?" At this point Guardo was standing beside her trying to know what was going on. She passed the phone to him so he could listen and then he handed it back to her with instruction to keep on talking with the caller. He went to the bedroom and picked up the extension.

The caller identified himself as a friend of James and Thomas who asked him to get in contact with her if ever, she found the diamond.

"How come you know I have found the diamond?"

"This is a small Island and news travel fast. Where can we meet?"

"What do you mean?" I do not have the diamond anymore so leave me alone."

"You have the name of the owner, don't you?"

"No, why would you think I would know the name of the owner, I gave the diamond to the police, and they will take care of it and just leave me alone."

"Settle down Missy, I just want to meet with you and talk about it."

"Who are you and why are you disguising your voice? Why would I want to talk with you, I do not know you?"

"Yes, you do."

And then the caller took his normal voice to continue the conversation.

"Thomas! Thomas where are you, the entire Island is looking for you. Why did you escape from prison?"

"I need some money to go away, far away."

At this point Guardo was standing beside her with the extension phone and making signals to her to invite him to meet her here.

"Ok, I will meet with you, where and when."

"Alone Andrea, no Officer Banji. Do you understand?"

Guardo made a gesture of yes to Andrea.

Ok, I will meet with you, when?"

"Tonight, meet me at the end of your beach where we were hiding in the tub."

"Ok, I will, what time?"

"Nine o'clock, alone."

"Nine o'clock, it is too dark at nine, I do not like walking on the beach that late."

"Andrea, nine o'clock." He screamed.

"Ok."

When nine o'clock came around Guardo was nervous to let her go alone.

"Listen, I will be alright, he used to love me remember."

"Don't remind me please."

"If it would make you happy, I will bring the dogs with me."

She kissed him and he returned her kiss with more passion, a few minutes later he let her go and she left on foot towards the end of the beach.

Thomas saw her coming down the beach with the dogs running back and forth and started to walk towards her. He stopped and she continued until she reached him.

"What do you want Thomas? Aren't you afraid of being caught by the police?"

"What, do you mean mousy Guardo, afraid of his shadow?'

"No, not Guardo but the entire force of police is looking for you, how can you be sure I did not call them."

"I don't know I just wanted to meet with you, maybe you can save me."

"How can I save you?"

"You can come with me to Canada, and we will live from the money James left you in New York."

"How do you know about the money James left me?"

"Dear Andrea, James was my friend for many years, we shared everything. He even gave me the green light if ever something would happen to him, I could put the moves on you."

"Put the moves on me. How generous of the bastard."

"Come on Andrea, you know you have feelings for me, remember our kiss."

"Excuse me! I had feelings for you, but they did not last long once I met the real you. I am in love with Guardo, he his twice the man of you two put together."

"Then you give me no choice but to kidnap you and demand a ransom."

"And you think I will let myself be kidnap!" She then pulled a gun on him.

"What, you would never shoot me?' He advanced slowly toward her, and the dogs started to growl at him.

"Brutus, it's me Thomas, come boy."

"You think Brutus will go to you know after abandoning him several times. Come Brutus, come Buddy." The dogs immediately obeyed her and came beside her.

Thomas screamed at the dogs as he made a gesture towards her, and she pulled the trigger and shot just past him.

"You bitch, you shot at me."

"I told you I would and next time I won't miss."

He started swearing at her as he advanced again towards her when she pulled the trigger, this time the bullet grazed his shoulder and he stop and fell to the ground.

"Do not come closer and you better leave or give yourself up to the police."

"Are you crazy and pass the next several years in prison. No thank you."

"I think you do not have the choice look behind you."

Guardo was coming down the hill and the dogs went to his side.

"The cavalry, Oh, I am scared. He laughs and then he saw three officers coming the opposite way, behind Andrea.

"You think I am stupid or what, I would meet with you without protection, come on Thomas were you banking on me being in love with you and run away with you to another country. Now who is the crazy one?"

He started to run towards the water and the dogs followed him, jumping after him thinking he wanted to play with them, and they almost drowned him.

A few minutes later the policemen had him handcuff and took him away. Andrea and Guardo walked back to the house slowly hand in hand with the two dogs running in front of them.

Later that month Thomas was trial for keeping information regarding several murder cases and was sent to prison for several years for other implications such as steeling and selling precious treasurers from sinking ships. James and Thomas were partners for several years and Andrea was cleared of all accusations.

A few months later, when all the individuals responsible for the murders of James, Mr. and Mrs. Santos were arrested, Andrea and Guardo were married in front of all their friends and family.

After everyone had left Andrea and Guardo went for a long walk on the beach talking about their future together.

"Look in the sky! How perfect, and she started.

"Star Light Star bright,
The first star I see tonight,
I wish I may, I wish I might,
Have the wish I wish tonight."

She closed her eyes and he waited…
"My love, what did you wish for?"
"To be happy as I am today for the rest of my life."
He smiled and they return inside the house for an evening both will never forget.

Later for their honeymoon they took the yacht for a long trip up to New York City with the two dogs and the cat to visit their Condo. Andrea was also allowed to keep the Mercedes, the yacht, and the land at the end of the beach and Brutus, Thomas' dog. They returned home three months later to their house on the beach to start a full and happy life together.

The end.